WESTERN UNION
SYMBOLS
CFI 63-Cable-C.D.Aml Jef Via Western Union. Feb.28th. 5:50 P.M.
Denis Pesey.
Jefferson,S.C.
Loving birthday greetings I wish we were together
on this special occasion with all my best wishes
for a speedy reunion letter sent.
Robert Pesey.
UNITED STATES POST OFFICE, PANAMA CITY, FLA.
46694

The Big Bout

TENNESSEE HOUSE
THEATRE
THEATRE
SOUTH OF DIXIE
SHORT NEWS
THEATRE

Books by Michael Lister

(John Jordan Novels)
Power in the Blood
Blood of the Lamb
Flesh and Blood
The Body and the Blood
Blood Sacrifice
Rivers to Blood
Blood Money
Blood Moon

(Short Story Collections)
North Florida Noir
Florida Heat Wave
Delta Blues
Another Quiet Night in Desparation

(Remington James novels)
Double Exposure
Separation Anxiety

(Merrick McKnight novels)
Thunder Beach
A Certain Retribution

(Jimmy "Soldier" Riley novels)
The Big Goodbye
The Big Beyond
The Big Hello
The Big Bout

(Sam Michaels and Daniel Davis Series)
Burnt Offerings
Separation Anxiety

The Big Bout

Michael Lister

a novel

PULPWOOD PRESS

Panama City, FL

Inquiries should be addressed to:
Pulpwood Press
P.O. Box 35038
Panama City, FL 32412

Lister, Michael.
The Big Bout / Michael
Lister.
-----1st ed.
p. cm.
ISBN: 978-1888146-51-6 (hardback)
ISBN: 978-1-888146-52-3 (trade paperback)

Library of Congress Control Number:

Book Design by Adam Ake

Printed in the United States

1 3 5 7 9 10 8 6 4 2

First Edition

For Aaron Bearden

For collaboration.

For conversation.

For humor.

For music, movies, and books.

For friendship.

Thank you

Dawn Lister, Jill Mueller,
Adam Ake, Micah Lister,
Aaron Bearden, Lou Columbus

Chapter 1

"It's tomorrow," Lauren said.

It was how she greeted me each morning.

Having promised each other to be together tomorrow and tomorrow and tomorrow without knowing how many we'd actually get, each morning when she opened her eyes she softly spoke those two words.

She had opened her eyes to find me lying on my side in the bed next to her, watching her sleep, listening to the sweet sound of her breathing.

"It is," I said.

The room was cold, but the bed was warm, our naked bodies beneath the blanket radiating heat.

"How many does that make?" she asked.

"Thought we were going to take each one as it comes," I said.

"I know, but . . ."

"Do you know what today is?" I asked.

She shook her head.

"It's Christmas."

"Is it?"

"Our first together."

"Merry Christmas," she said.

"Merry Christmas yourself."

"This is the best Christmas ever," she said.

She was right. We were both banged up pretty bad. We were in a small, cold hotel room because we had nowhere else to go. We were penniless. We had no prospects. We were facing a future that broke toward the bleak. But we were together, finally and forever, and it was the best Christmas by far I had ever experienced.

This past year had been a turning point in the war. Our victories in Stalingrad, North Africa, and Sicily were cause for hope.

Last night in each other's arms, Lauren and I had listened to President Roosevelt's Christmas Eve radio address.

Some of what he said still echoed in my ears.

"On this Christmas Eve there are over ten million men in the armed forces of the United States alone. One year ago, 1,700,000 were serving overseas. Today, this figure has been more than doubled to 3,800,000 on duty overseas. By next July first that number overseas will rise to over 5,000,000 men and women . . .

"But—on Christmas Eve this year—I can say to you that at last we may look forward into the future with real, substantial confidence that, however great the cost, 'peace on earth, good will toward men' can be and will be realized and ensured. This year I can say that. Last year I could not do more than express a hope. Today I express—a certainty, though the cost may be high and the time may be long . . .

"Within the past year—within the past few weeks—history has been made, and it is far better history for the whole human race than any that we have known, or even dared to hope for, in these tragic times through which we pass . . .

"Tonight, on Christmas Eve, all men and women everywhere who love Christmas are thinking of that ancient town and of the star of faith that shone there more than nineteen centuries ago. American boys are fighting today in snow-covered mountains, in malarial jungles, and on blazing deserts, they are fighting on the far stretches of the sea and above the clouds, and fighting for the thing for which they struggle. I think it is best symbolized by the message that came out of Bethlehem.

"On behalf of the American people—your own people—I send this Christmas message to you, to you who are in our armed forces: In our hearts are prayers for you and for all your comrades in arms who fight to rid the world of evil. We ask God's blessing upon you—upon your fathers, and mothers, and wives, and children—all your loved ones at home. We ask that the comfort of God's grace shall be granted to those who are sick and wounded, and to those who are prisoners of war in the hands of the enemy, waiting for the day when they will again be free.

"And we ask that God receive and cherish those who have given their lives, and that He keep them in honor and in the grateful memory of their countrymen forever. God bless all of you who fight our battles on this Christmas Eve. God bless us all. Keep us strong in our faith that we fight for a better day for humankind—here and everywhere."

I carefully eased what was remaining of my right arm beneath Lauren's neck, wrapped my left around her too-thin torso and slid toward her, even as I pulled her closer to me, her bare breasts softly pressing against my chest, her dark hair cascading down around us, and kissed her gently on her full, warm lips. Toes and tongues and sex touching.

Reaching down between us, she took me in her hand.

"It's tomorrow," she said.

"It is."

"And it's Christmas."

"It is."

"It's time," she said.

"Are you sure?"

We had waited. She had told me repeatedly that she was ready but she seemed so frail I was afraid I'd—

"I won't break," she said.

You're already broken, I thought. *We both are.*

It was the first time we made love since we had plunged into the deep, dark abyss, since I had lost my arm, since she had gotten so sick, since we had lost and found each other over and over, since we had died and come back to life again.

Before she came back to me I thought I'd never be able to make love again—and not just because I had no desire to make love to anyone but her, but because of my injuries. Since she had, like Lazarus, returned from the grave to me, I had no doubt that if given the opportunity I would be able to demonstrate to her my great love for her.

Inside her I felt as I always did, as I did only when inside her, as if I were connected to all of creation and that I was meant to be.

She felt for me like the only home I'd truly ever have.

Back in October, Bing Crosby had recorded "I'll Be Home for Christmas" for soldiers serving overseas, lonely young men longing to be with their loved ones. During the past month or so I had played the 78rpm Decca Records single over and over and thought of Lauren, thought of us, never dreaming we'd be together when Christmas finally came.

The song would forever be our song, and I could hear it as we made love.

Christmas Eve will find me

Where the love light gleams

As I climaxed and fought the urge to collapse on top of her, she whispered, "Merry Christmas, darling."

Later, lying in bed, her body draped over mine, she said, "I honestly didn't think we were ever going to get to do that again."

"Me either."

"I think it's better because of that."

I nodded.

"God, I'm grateful," she said.

"*You*?" I said, my voice rising. "Lady, let me tell you somethin'—"

The tap at the door stopped me.

I waited. Only two people in the entire war-torn world knew we were here—Clip and the night manager—neither of whom should be knocking because both of whom were supposed to be out of town.

The tap came again. This time more insistent.

I slid out of bed and into my clothes, grabbing my gun out of its holster as I did.

Easing over to the door, I said, "Who is it?"

"A nigger and a Jap," Clip said. "Let us in before we get our asses shot out here."

"Merry Christmas, boss," Miki said.

She was carefully carrying a couple of covered dishes.

Miki Matsumoto had big, black, shy eyes the shape of almonds beneath her bangs, a cute oval face, and flawless porcelain skin. The corners of her eyes were still slightly discolored, but most of the bruising, abrasions, and swelling was now gone.

Clip came in behind her, a huge smile on his face.

"Merry Christmas, Miki," I said. "And I'm not your boss."

Lauren was dressed and sitting up in the bed looking breathtaking.

"I cook Japanese Christmas dinner for you and Mrs. Lady Boss."

"She insisted," Clip said. "Knew y'all needed to eat. Kinda curious to see what a Japanese Christmas dinner look like."

Lauren looked at me, her eyebrows raised, her face a bemused question mark.

I explained.

Miki Matsumoto was a beautiful Japanese teen who, after having escaped the Japanese-American internment camp near Manzanar with her family, had been abducted, beaten, and repeatedly raped while they were hiding on Panama City Beach.

I had found her and returned her to her mother and uncle, but she had shown up at my office a few days ago, cleaned it to within an inch of its life, and said she worked for me now.

"I am disgrace," Miki said. "Defiled. No man want me but dirty old man. Family make me marry him. Say it only op . . ."

"Option," Clip said.

"Op-tion for me now. But I not go back. I work for Soldier Jimmy now."

"I'm Lauren," she said, extending her hand. "It's nice to meet you."

"Miki. Miki Matsumoto," she said, bowing slightly. "I be very good worker for your husband-san. Keep both eye on him for you. Help him help other poor soul like me."

Lauren smiled and nodded. "Thank you."

"Let's eat," Clip said.

We did—Miki and Lauren on the bed, Clip and I standing next to the chest of drawers.

The food was different than any I'd ever had, but was good and warming on the cold December day. It began with a paste-based soup that included a salty blend of soybeans, carrots, potatoes, and a few ingredients I didn't recognize. We then had a small bowl of rice, followed by fish and vegetables.

Each of the others held their small bowls with one hand and ate with the other. I had to eat by placing my bowl on top of the chest of drawers and leaning down over it.

"This is very good, Miki," Lauren said.

"It really is," I said. "Thank you very much for feeding us on this cold Christmas morning."

"It is for honor," she said, and bowed slightly.

"She got the job?" Clip asked.

"I cook and clean," Miki said. "I learn English and come good sec-re-tary."

"Miki, your uncle and his men will be watching my office—and even if they weren't . . . if anyone reported you . . . you'd be sent back to an internment camp. But mostly . . . I don't even know that I'm going to reopen the agency or if I can even make a go of it if I did. Do you understand?"

"Lady Boss Lauren help Miki with . . . with dis . . ." She trailed off and looked over at Clip.

"Disguise," he said.

He spoke to her more gently and with more patience than I'd ever heard him speak to anyone except his mom and sister.

"Disguise," she said. "No one know I Jap bastard."

We all laughed at that.

"And I help make you man much success. Save many like Miki."

I looked over at Lauren.

She nodded and smiled. "Lady Boss Lauren is in."

This time when Miki bowed toward her, Lauren bowed back.

"Nowa that settle," Miki said, "we get to business down. We not bring lunch and new Jap bastard secretary but new case along for you."

I looked over at Clip.

"You heard about that big boxing bout on the eleventh?"

I nodded.

On January 11, 1944—during the radio broadcast of the President's State of the Union Address to Congress, a heavyweight bout with political, social, and title ramifications was being staged in an outdoor venue downtown at the foot of Harrison Avenue near the USO Club.

The plan was for the radio transmission of the President's speech to be blasted through loudspeakers in and around the arena during the fight and for the bout to raise money for the war effort.

"It a big deal," he said. "Winner could get a shot at Joe after the war."

Joe was Joe Louis, the Brown Bomber, who had been heavyweight champ since June 22, 1937 when he knocked out the Cinderella Man, Jim Braddock, in the eighth round in Chicago.

"You really think there will be an *after* to all this?"

Lauren said.

"The challenger gettin' death threats. Manager want to hire us to protect him and figure out who behind it."

"Us?"

"You and me. Riley-Jones Detective Agency."

I laughed. "How's he even know about this non-existent agency?"

"Challenger my cousin."

"Fighting Freddy Freeman is your cousin?" Lauren said.

"Well, we pretty sure we got the same daddy . . . so whatever that make us."

"That was very nice of you, Lady Boss Lauren," I said.

She smiled.

"What we're doing to Japanese-Americans is dreadful. We can't help everyone, but we can help her."

I thought about how eager Miki was to be my secretary and it reminded me of July, the agency's last secretary, who had been killed on the job. Was I setting up Miki for the same fate?

"I'll help," she said. "So will Clip. It won't be like it was with July."

I gave her a guilty smile.

"That is what you were thinking, isn't it? I could see it in your eyes. Everything's not on you. Not anymore. We're together. We'll face everything together. Me at your side. A full partner in this. In everything."

I nodded.

"I mean it. I'm getting better every day. I'm gonna be able to pull my weight. I promise."

"I know."

"You don't, but it's true."

"I believe you."

"Soldier, we have each other. We have everything."

"We do."

"We have to help others have . . . if not everything . . . at least something."

"We will."

"We should start by riding over to Oak Cove and bringing Christmas cheer to Gladys," she said. "She has no one."

"*We*? You feel up to that?"

We drove out of the Cove, down Beach Drive toward Beck.

The world appeared abandoned, its inhabitants rounded up and removed. No cars. No people. No signs of human life at all. Of course, I knew it wasn't the world nor even the entire town, but so complete was the Christmas cloistering that it felt like the vanishing applied to far more than just the street we were on.

On Beach we passed the huge house Lauren had shared with her husband Harry.

She looked away from it, casting her gaze across the street and out onto the cold, calm bay.

"You okay?" I asked.

She nodded slowly, lips pursed, brow furrowed, eyes narrowed in consideration.

"How could I have been so . . . stupid, so naive, so . . ."

"You weren't. You were a child. He saved you. Started working on you way back then."

"But—"

"And it was only out of your incredible sense of

guilt and obligation and loyalty—to your family as much as Harry—that he was able to exploit you the way he did."

"I just feel so foolish, like such a silly little school girl."

"You're not. Sorry you feel that way. But you're not. *I* was the fool."

"You?"

"Sure. For what I believed about you. For how I betrayed you, what I did to you."

"You saved me. Then you saved my life. You—"

"Dress it up however you like, sister. I was the fool. And one of my own making. 'Love is not love which alters when it alteration finds.'"

She turned slightly but suddenly, snatching her gaze away from the bay, looking directly at me with intent and intensity. "*I love you*," she said. At that moment, her mouth was an organ of fire, her vocal chords vibrating flames, her three small words containing an infinite amount of passion and compassion, appreciation and affection. "And you didn't falter when you thought I had."

"The things I believed about you, the way I hated . . ."

"It wasn't hate," she said. "It was love. Wounded, suffering, hurting, bleeding love. Your love for me was still your ever-fixed mark."

"*Fixated*," I said.

She smiled.

We passed by the ornate, opulent, and lushly landscaped Oak Cove and I thought of Gladys all alone in her hospital bed—the way her husband of over thirty years was in a different room in a different building across town, and it made me sad. *Life is loss*, I thought. We lose everything eventually, everything in the end.

We found Gladys slumped in a rocking chair next to her bed in her small, mostly empty room.

She wore a wrinkled housecoat over simple men's cotton pajamas that must have belonged to Henry.

Her white hair was shorter and thinner than I remembered, her skin more pale and wrinkled.

She was dozing, her eyes moving beneath her closed lids, her soft breaths coming out in small airy sounds she'd be self-conscious of if she could hear them.

As we stepped into the small cell like room, I was overcome with a profound sadness—and not just for Gladys, but for us all.

Unbidden, images of an elderly, lonely Lauren slumped in just such a chair in just such a room forced their way into my mind.

It all comes to this, I thought. *And that's if we make it this far at all.*

Gladys blinked a few times, opened her eyes, and smiled up at us.

As usual, she had a gentle, sweet, pleasant expression on her face—the kind only the truly good and guileless are capable of.

"*Jimmy*," she exclaimed.

I smiled at her and took her hand.

"Merry Christmas, Miss Gladys," Lauren said, taking her other hand.

"Christmas?" she asked, confused. "Is it really? But I haven't done my shopping. I don't—"

"We did it for you," Lauren said. "We took care of everything. Just like you wanted."

"Who are you?"

"I'm Lauren."

"That's right. *Lauren.* Oh Lauren, I'm sorry. Sometimes I forget things."

"It's okay. We all do."

"And who is this handsome young man with you?" Gladys asked, looking back at me.

"That's Jimmy. He used to work with Henry."

"Who?"

Lauren looked at me.

"What happened to your arm?" Gladys asked.

"Just a little accident," I said. "It's okay. We're just so glad to be here with you today. We love you very much."

The mask of confusion left her face and she smiled up at me.

Her blue eyes seemed sunken and faded somehow, and a little lost in the excessive fluid of their sockets, but warmth and genuine generosity could still be seen in them.

"I love y'all too. I really do. Now . . . who were y'all again?"

"Jimmy and Lauren," I said.

"Jimmy, that's right. You're . . . my . . . son. Is that right?"

I nodded and smiled.

"That's right, darling," Henry Folsom said as he haltingly walked into the room. "He's the closest thing we've ever had to a son."

Her face brightened. "Henry," she said with unguarded affection, her soft, misshapen mouth forming an unrestrained smile.

I stiffened and stood upright, angry adrenaline arcing through me.

Lauren took my hand.

"Well," she said, "we've got to go now but we sure hope you have a very merry Christmas."

"Is it Christmas?" Gladys asked.

"It is," Folsom said. "December twenty-fifth, nineteen-forty-three."

I leaned down, lifted the cold, bony hand I was holding, and kissed it gently. "Merry Christmas," I said. "We'll see you soon."

"Is it Christmas again already?" she asked.

We said goodbye and turned to walk out, never even acknowledging Folsom's presence as we did.

"I'll be right back, honey," Folsom said.

"Where are you going?"

"Let me just see them out. Won't take but a minute."

"What?"

"I'll be right back."

"Okay. I'll be right here. I'm Gladys by the way. Pleased to make your acquaintance."

We were several feet down the hallway when Henry Folsom emerged from his wife's room and began slowly following us.

"Jimmy," he said.

We kept walking.

"Jimmy. Please. I can't catch you. Please stop for a moment."

Lauren squeezed my hand and we stopped and turned toward him.

It took a moment, but he finally caught up to us.

"Lauren, it's so good to see you up and about. You

look like you're doing good."

"Doing much better than I would be if you had had your way," she said.

"I owe you both an apology. Things got out of hand. I got caught up in something that I thought I could control, but . . . I was wrong and I'm so sorry. I'm so glad you're both okay. I really, truly am. And it means the world to me that you came to see my Gladys today."

"Thought you were still in the hospital," I said. "Thought she was alone."

"Just got out. Decided to disobey doctors' orders and just leave. Couldn't be away from her another minute. She doesn't know who I am most of the time, but . . . it seems to help her . . . just not being alone."

"I'd be happy to come sit with her some when you can't," Lauren said.

"You would? Really?"

"She had nothing to do with what you did or tried to do to us."

She has everything to do with it, I thought. *She's the reason he did it.*

"That would be . . ." he began, but his voice broke and he began to cry. "Thank you so much. I'm so sorry. Please find it in your hearts to forgive me and let me find a way to make it up to you."

"Imprisonment and attempted rape and murder and selling someone into sexual slavery aren't really things you can make up for," I said.

"No, I guess they aren't," he said. "When you say it like that . . . I guess . . . we never know what we're actually capable of, do we?"

I thought about what I had done to get Lauren back,

what I had found I was capable of, and what it had cost me.

"Some of us know what we're *not*," Lauren said.

She was standing up to power. Her voice was strong and steady.

We were all quiet a moment. It was the closest he had come to admitting his part in our nightmare.

I recalled reading something Dostoyevsky wrote. *Nothing is easier than to denounce the evildoer; nothing is more difficult than to understand him.*

Could I understand Henry? Was I him?

"Then why would you … help . . . me . . . with—"

"I'm helping her," Lauren said. "Got nothing to do with you."

He nodded, and we turned and walked away without another word.

Chapter 4

"Joe Louis ain't gonna be champion forever," Saul Behr said.

"You sure?" I asked.

It wasn't just that Louis had been champion for going on six years. It was the way he had dominated the division, outclassing every challenger by margins so wide as to seem something from the movies. His title defenses before the war had been so often and so one-sided, sports writers took to calling Joe's challengers the Bum of the Month Club.

He smiled. Something he did often and easily, as if he found nearly everything amusing.

Saul Behr was a trim sixty-something man with dark, intelligent eyes that sparked with equal parts deviousness and delight. His olive skin was only a little lined and what gray hair he had was thin and wispy.

"I'm pretty sure," he said. "I'll tell you something else too. The war ain't gonna go on forever neither."

"You sure?" I asked.

"Of all the contenders I've seen . . . Freddy has the best chance to be the next world champion."

"Okay."

"I ain't the only one who thinks it. He's attracting attention."

"And getting death threats," I said.

"You know how many people would like Joe Louis dead? He's as non-threatening as a Negro heavyweight could be. Always says and does the right thing in public. Follows the rules. Hell, he's helpin' win the war. Raising all kind of funds through charity bouts. Remember what he said when he enlisted and they asked him his occupation? He said, 'Fighting, and let us at them Japs.' Says things like 'We'll win, 'cause we're on God's side.' And lots of people still want him dead."

I remembered reading how Joe's management actually gave him a list of rules to follow. Things like never have his picture taken with a white woman, never gloat over a fallen opponent, never engage in fixed fights, live and fight clean. And as far as I could tell, Joe had followed them all.

Boxing, a sport I had loved and followed since childhood, was blighted by betting, marred by corruption. Joe Louis, America's first Negro hero, had not only avoided the taint of turpitude, but had restored the nation's faith in the sport.

Joe was a gracious and graceful champion, and carried himself with as much dignity as anyone in professional sports ever had.

"You know why Joe's so careful?" Saul asked. "Why his public image is so pristine?"

I nodded. "In addition to all the other reasons," I said, "Jack Johnson."

"Black Jack Johnson," he said, smiling and nodding.

Joe Louis was not the first Negro heavyweight champion of the world. That distinction belonged to the Gavelston Giant, Jack Johnson. Everything Louis was not—or would not let himself be in public—Johnson was. Flashy. Flamboyant. Unapologetic. Controversial. Notorious. He had held the title from December 1908 until April 1915 and been the most famous and hated Negro in the country at the time—maybe the world.

During a time of racial segregation and second-class citizenship for Negroes, Jack Johnson was written about and photographed more than just about anybody in the country. He was vilified and demonized by whites and didn't care—which bothered them all the more. At a time when it was not only illegal but deadly for a black man to be in a relationship with a white woman, Johnson defiantly dated and even married them.

"Even with all Joe's done, even with how quiet and polite and differential, he's still hated and some people will always want him dead—or at least not champ."

I knew from my many close calls with Clip the extent to which white people misunderstood, feared, and hated black people in general and black men in particular. It was sad and sick, a national disease that was particularly acute in the South.

In perhaps the most important sporting event in human history, Joe had fought for his country, had taken on Hitler and the Nazis not once but twice, when he stepped into the ring against Max Schmeling.

Joe fought Schmeling the first time in June of '36. The fight, which was supposed to be more of a tune-up than anything else before Joe got his shot at the title, followed hard on the heels of his being named Athlete of the Year by the Associated Press. Schmeling, a former champion, had won his title on a technicality when Jack Sharkey had been disqualified for a low blow, and was not considered a threat to the number-one contender. Perhaps because of this, Joe didn't train as hard as he might have, opting to spend more time on the golf course than in the gym.

Not so with Max. He not only trained intensely, but prepared carefully, actually obtaining the film of Joe fighting Paulino Uzcudun and studying it so thoroughly that he found a weakness in Joe's style. Joe had a habit of dropping his left hand after he jabbed—something Max exploited in the process of handing Joe his first professional loss by knocking him out in the twelfth round.

Schmeling's shocking victory over Louis was used by the Nazis as confirmation of their racial superiority and as part of their enormous propaganda machine—something Schmeling wanted no part of.

After defeating Louis, Schmeling expected a title shot against James J. Braddock, who had also won a shocking upset by defeating Max Baer for the heavyweight title, but behind the scenes Joe and Jim's managers worked out a deal that led to a Braddock-Louis matchup instead of a Braddock-Schmeling one.

When Joe beat Braddock and became world champion, it set up possibly the most important prizefight in history—a rematch with Schmeling.

Because the Nazi party had so successfully used Schmeling's defeat of Louis as a symbol of Aryan superiority, the rematch took on significant political implications. When Joe visited the White House a few weeks before the bout, the President told him, "Joe, we need muscles like yours to beat Germany."

The political ramifications of the fight only intensified when Nazi party publicists accompanying Schmeling in New York for the rematch issued statements such as a black man could not defeat a German, and that Schmeling's winnings would be used to build tanks for Germany.

In the fevered buildup for the rematch, Schmeling's hotel was picketed by anti-Nazi protesters and the entire world was watching.

The fight took place the night of June 22, 1938, in Yankee Stadium in front of a crowd of over seventy thousand. Millions more around the world tuned in by radio.

Unlike the previous bout, Joe took the rematch seriously and trained intensely, later remarking, "I knew I had to get Schmeling good. I had my own personal reasons and the whole damned country was depending on me."

He came into the fight weighing just under 199 pounds—six more than Max.

The fight only lasted two minutes.

The Brown Bomber battered Schmeling from the beginning, forcing him to the ropes and finishing him with a devastating body blow.

Joe knocked Schmeling down three times and allowed him to throw only two punches during the entire assault.

After the third knockdown, Schmeling's trainer threw in the towel and the referee called a halt to the fight.

"The thing is," Saul said, "Freddy . . . Freddy's no Joe Louis. He's cut from the same unapologetically dark cloth as Black Jack Johnson. He's smart and angry and outspoken. And he scares the shit out of most whites. And someone wants him dead before he ever gets the chance to be champ."

"But is this bout that important?" I asked. "I thought it was just an exhibition match. More for fundraising than anything else."

"It was," he said. "But Gentleman Jeff Bennett backed out and the number one contender in the world, Leonaldo Lights Out Linderman, has stepped in to take his place. If Freddy beats Leonaldo, he'll get a shot at Joe."

Gentleman Jeff Bennett was known as the world's only boxing war correspondent, and though he was a better reporter than boxer, he was a hell of a good boxer.

"What happened to Bennett?" I asked.

"He disappeared. Don't know any details. I'm sure there will be those that say I had something to do with it, but I didn't. And neither did Freddy. Truth is, I'd'a preferred he have a few more fights before facing Linderman, but . . . I'll have him ready."

Chapter 5

I wasn't prepared for how much like Clip his half brother would look.

Except for the two good eyes and extra weight and muscle, Fighting Freddy Freeman could be Clipper Jones's doppelgänger.

"Damn he a good-lookin' nigger," Clip said.

We were standing in the gym of Bay High School watching Freddy spar in a ring that had been set up for that reason.

The temporary training facility, consisting of a boxing ring, heavy and speed bags, weights, and other exercise equipment, was used by both fighters at different times—though Linderman wasn't utilizing it nearly as often as Freddy.

"Huh, what'd I tell you?" Saul Behr said coming up from behind us. "Kid has somethin', don't he?"

"Yeah," Clip said, "astonishing good looks."

"He's quick, tough, smart," Saul said. "Fights defensively. Hard as hell to hit, but he's got one hell of a beard on him too. He might get beat but he ain't gonna get beat up. Or knocked out. Just ain't gonna happen."

I nodded and continued watching.

Freddy was fast and though he was outclassing his opponent, I wasn't sure he had the skills to beat anybody other than a sparring partner. At five feet ten inches and one hundred and eighty-five pounds, Freddy was smallish for the division ruled by the Brown Bomber, who stood two inches over six feet and weighed in at just under two hundred pounds.

"But his real secret is his punchin' power. Both hands too. He catches you with that overhand right or short left hook . . . and . . . it'll be night-night for Lights Out."

"All that may be true," Clip said, "but I just can't get over how goddamn good lookin' he be."

As if on cue, Freddy drove a crushing straight hand right flush into the face of his opponent, which even with headgear on felled the fighter. He hit the canvas and didn't get up.

It was an impressive punch, but one he'd have a very difficult time getting through the guard of a skilled boxer. And he'd probably get a taste of the canvas for even trying.

"Dammit Freddy," Saul yelled. "I told you to stop doing that. You're gonna run out of fighters willing to spar with you, and then what?"

"Clip'll always climb in with me," Freddy said.

"See?" Saul said to us. "He's good, right?"

"Knocked hell outta his sparring partner," Clip said. "Ain't no denying that."

After helping the fallen boxer up, Freddy ducked between the ropes, climbed down from the ring, and walked over to where we were, using his mouth to unlace his gloves as he did.

Unlike his sparring partner, Freddy wore no

headgear.

"Clipper Jones," he said. "Nigger, you lookin' like a bag of bones up in them clothes. Nobody feedin' you?"

Actually, Clip had begun to fill out a little lately—probably the result of Miki's cooking. If Freddy thought he looked bad now, he should've seen him just a week or so back.

Rivulets of sweat snaked down Freddy's dark, muscular body in long serpentine trails, and his breathing was slightly elevated from exertion. His gray boxing trunks were damp but not soaked through and he appeared to have on no socks beneath his boxing boots.

"Freddy, this is the fella I was tellin' you about. Meet Jimmy Riley."

He extended his gloved hand. When I tapped it with my left, he noticed for the first time I was missing most of my right.

"Saul, you crazy Jew bastard. Quit clownin' around. Shee-it, bringin' me a one-armed bodyguard. You're a funny man."

Freddy finally managed to get the gloves off, which he promptly grabbed by the wrist ends and began tapping his leg with.

"Freddy, it's no joke. He's who we're hiring to—"

"Oh, 'cause a nigger's life only worth half a—"

"It ain't like that," Saul said. "You know that. I'm always looking out for you. Come on. Clip'll tell you."

"Nobody tellin' me anything that'll convince me to hire a one-armed bodyguard."

"Freddy, shut the fuck up," Clip said. "Jimmy the best I ever seen—better than any two-armed motherfuckers you can find. He who I'd want guardin' me."

“Yeah, well, you ain’t got no shot at the title, do you?”

“You ain’t got much of one from what I just seen,” Clip said.

Freddy looked at me. “What you think? He right?”

“About you, yeah. You’re fast and you got punchin’ power, but those’ll only get you so far.”

“I meant about you,” he said. “Wasn’t askin’ no one-armed white boy for boxin’ advice. Don’t care what kind of war hero he is.”

I shook my head. “I’m not the best. Not even close.”

“He said you the best he seen, but he only got one eye. And it ain’t so good, I guess. Who the best you’ve seen?”

“Pinkerton named Parker and a shooter named Burke.”

“Get me one of them,” he said to Freddy.

“He can’t,” Clip said. “They no longer with us. Know why? ’Cause Jimmy here pine-boxed ’em both.”

I honestly had not thought of that when I said their names. It wasn’t something I was proud of. In fact, the way in which I had killed one of them was among the lowest things I had ever done. It was a source of shame and embarrassment. My response to his question had just been an immediate and honest one—they were the two best shooters I had ever seen.

“Now, your dumb ass was gonna get both of us risking our lives to protect you and find out who behind this for . . .” He turned his head slightly toward me. “How much were we gonna get for this shit?”

“Five dollars a day,” I said.

“Five fuckin’ dollars a day,” Clip said.

"Plus expenses," Saul added.

"Plus expenses," Clip said. "And that 'cause I was doin' it for you and Jimmy was doin' it for me, but you too stupid a nigger to see what you bein' offered."

Clip turned to leave and I followed.

"You only got three eyes and arms between you," Freddy yelled behind us.

Chapter 6

"Nigger know better," Clip said.

We had just emerged from the Bay High gymnasium and were walking toward the car, which was parked on Harrison.

The traffic was still wartime heavy, even during the holidays, and down the way, random servicemen in uniform were walking along the sidewalk toward downtown.

"He wasn't wrong," I said.

"About?"

"Anything. We do only have three arms and eyes between us."

"I meant—"

"You'd act the same way if he'd've brought a one-armed man to be your bodyguard."

"He know better than not to trust me."

I nodded. "There is that."

As we neared the car, I noticed another one, a nondescript black Ford, pull up and park on the corner.

Above us, the fronds of planted palm trees clacked together in the coldish December wind.

"From what I saw, he's no threat to the belt," I said.

"Why would anyone who knows anything about boxin' think he is?"

Two men got of the car and headed toward the gym. Even from a distance it was obvious the men were enormous, even elephantine in every way.

They weren't wearing signs that identified them as local muscle, but they might as well have. Both big. Both dressed in ill-fitting black suits. Both with dark, closely cropped hair. The body language of both that of bullies, of men on a mission with no regard for anyone or anything else.

The massive men moved with the speed and agility of beached manatees.

"He mostly play possum when he train in there," Clip was saying. "Never know who watching. That was all just bullshit. 'Cept for the knockout. That for our benefit."

"He makes for a convincing possum," I said.

"Do, don't he?"

I nodded toward the two mammoth men nearing the gym. Clip turned and eyed them.

"What happened to the gym?" Clip said. "It was just there."

"It's behind them," I said.

Without saying another word, we both began jogging back toward the building.

"Saul, how's your nigger gonna fight if only one hand works?" one of the gargantuan guys was saying.

The other had the fingers of Freddy's right hand bent back to the point of breaking.

"I could teach him," I said.

As both of the big men turned to look at me, I could see that they were twins.

One of the giants and Saul were standing not far from where we walked in. The other, the one threatening to snap Freddy's wrist, was over closer to the ring. Freddy's trainer, a thin, quiet elderly black man named Gus, stood nearby.

"Big bastards are twins," Clip said. "Bet they blew the bottom out of they mama. I mean . . . gotdamn. No way bitch ever walk normal again."

"The fuck?" the big man closest to Saul said.

"He's referring to your size," I explained, "and the fact that there are two of you and the toll that must have taken on your poor mother."

"She a big woman?" Clip asked.

Before the big man could respond, Clip closed the distance between them, withdrawing his weapon as he did, and now had it pointed at his huge head.

"You're makin' a big mistake, mister," the man said.

His voice was thick and slow and a little gargly—as if his vocal chords were being squeezed together by the fat in his neck.

"Tell your brother to let Freddy go," Clip said.

His brother did it without being told.

"This is just business," the big man said to Clip. "Got nothin' to do with you. Tell 'em, Freddy."

"Yeah," Clip said, "tell us, Freddy."

"I don't know what the fat bastard talkin' about," Freddy said.

We all stepped forward and converged around Clip, Saul, and the man who made Clip's big gun look small.

"What kind of business you in?" I asked.

"We ain't in business," the other brother said. "But the man we work for is."

"Why doesn't he want Freddy to fight?" I asked.

"He does."

"Wonder what the fuck would come out of his fat head if I pulled the trigger?" Clip asked.

It seemed a random question he was genuinely curious about at the moment.

"Listen," the twin without the gun pressed to his forehead said, "you do anything to either of us and you'll bring down hell on your heads like you can't imagine. Put your gun away. Let us walk. Nobody gets hurt today."

"Who do you work for?" I asked.

"A very discreet man who doesn't like drawing attention to himself," he said.

"That were true," I said, "he would not employ you two."

"I really want to see what comes out of his head," Clip said. "Think it be jelly or custard or just like lard?"

"Tell them to let us go, Freddy," the brother Clip was holding said.

"Man, let him go," Freddy said. "Let 'em walk."

Clip looked at me. "Did that sound like an order to you?"

I nodded.

"I just meant . . . Clip man, come on. We don't need this kind of trouble."

"Oh, you prefer the kind where they break your hand?"

"Clip, this some serious shit. You don't understand. Please. Just let 'em go. Okay? Please."

"We should be dead," Lauren said.

"We were," I said.

She nodded. "You're right. Actually, *we were.*"

What if we still are?

Where had that come from?

If we are, then we're more alive in death than we ever were in life.

She didn't say anything else right away, and we just sat with the truth of it for a moment.

We had just made love—something we were doing as often as possible these days—and were still in bed.

I was leaning on the headboard, propped on a few pillows. She was propped up on me, her head lying on my chest, an arm draped around my waist. We were both smoking, sharing a cigarette back and forth like it was the last on the planet. She had pulled it from the nearest pack and I had no idea what brand it was. I just knew sharing it with her made it, like everything, infinitely better.

Our lovemaking was so similar in so many ways, so different in others.

We had always hungered for the other with an

intensity and insatiability unparalleled in my experience. That remained the same. We had always made love as often as possible. That remained the same.

We were the same, yet so different. We now bore scars, seen and not, that had altered who we were as human beings, as a couple, as lovers.

Our first encounters were adulterous, unsanctioned, taboo. They were, by necessity, a secret, something stolen, something hidden, something all too brief and ultimately evanescent.

Now we were a couple. Each belonging to the other entirely and exclusively. We were unrushed, yet never completely unhurried. Now it wasn't others—husband, friends, society—but time itself that was a foe to our time together.

But of all the things that were different now, the single biggest was our palpable gratitude for every single sacred second we were given, like so many gifts from a generous and beneficent God.

"We're living on borrowed time," she said.

"Isn't everybody?"

She thought about it, then began nodding—slowly at first, then faster. "You're right. I guess they are."

Her dark hair was down, splayed out across my chest, and it swirled back and forth a bit as she nodded.

"Everybody is," I said. "Not everybody knows it. I didn't."

"Me either. But now I do . . ." she said, her voice trailing off.

"Me too."

"Now . . . I'm acutely aware of it. When I was dead to you . . . and you to me . . . I used to think . . . if I ever got the chance to see you again, to talk to you, to . . . to hold you . . . even for a moment, I'd . . . that I would never take it for granted, that I would know how fleeting, how fragile, how impossibly precious it was . . . it is."

I was reading a recent copy of *Ring Magazine* when Miki ushered Kay Hudson into my office.

I recognized her from the photograph that often accompanied her bylines. Kay Hudson was one of a very few female war correspondents—and one of the very best.

Tossing the magazine on my desk, I stood to greet her.

"I'm Kay Hudson," she said, extending her hand across my desk.

She hadn't noticed most of my right arm was missing yet, so she had reached for it.

I awkwardly extended my left over to find her hand and gave it an upside-down shake.

"Sorry, Soldier," she said. "I didn't—"

I waved off her apology. "No need to be. Have a seat, please."

"I leave you two to make arrangement," Miki said. "I right outside if you need me."

With that she turned, walked out, and closed the door.

"I'd like to hire you," Kay said.

"I'd like to be hired."

"A friend of mine is missing . . . I'd like you to find him."

I waited, nodding her toward telling me more.

"The things I've seen," she said, shaking her head, looking off into the distance, seeing something that wasn't there. "You can't imagine what people are capable of."

"I might be able to," I said.

Our eyes locked and stayed that way a moment, then she glanced at what was left of my right arm.

"Maybe you can," she said, returning her intense gaze back to me. "How bad was it for you over there?"

"The worst," I said. "Didn't get to go."

"Oh. Well, what happened?"

"I walked into a shotgun blast. What do you know about me?"

She started to say something, then stopped. "Well, nothing I suppose. Why?"

"Why hire me? What made you choose me?"

"Can I be honest with you?"

"I'm not sure," I said, "but I'd like to see."

"You're the only . . . person in your profession in town."

"That was good," I said. "Keep it up."

"I don't follow."

"Keep makin' with the honesty. I like it."

"Like I said, the things I've seen . . . the things we've survived over there . . . To make it home and then go missing . . . it's just too . . ."

"Who's missing?"

"Have you heard about the big boxing match that's coming up?"

"I've heard a thing or three."

"The man who is missing was supposed to be in it."

"Jeff Bennett?"

She nodded. "He's a colleague of mine. He and his wife both, actually. They're pretty famous for being one of the few couples reporting the war together."

Gentleman Jeff Bennett was famous for being the world's only boxing war correspondent, but was far more famous for being part of Jeff and Rebecca Bennett—a husband and wife team traveling the world and reporting the war.

"The things Jeff and Becky and I have been through, have survived over there. I just can't accept that he made it through all that only to come and have something happen to him here."

When I opened the door to my office for Kay Hudson to depart, I found Lauren waiting for me.

Instantly my day improved.

She was alone in the reception area, seated behind Miki's desk, legs crossed, hands folded, gloves and hat on the blotter, beautiful, elegant, even regal.

I quickly introduced the two women and ushered Kay out so I could be alone with Lauren.

"Is everything okay?" I asked after Kay was gone.

"Yes, fine," she said. "Just fine."

"Where's Miki?"

"You've got to start calling her by her office name," she said.

As part of her transformation and to help conceal her true identity and ethnicity, Miki had been christened Judy by Lauren, but it was too close to July—the name of our previous secretary—for me, and I had yet to start using it.

"Judy is in the little lady's room. She'll be back in a bit."

She stood and we made our way into my office,

leaving the door open until Miki's return, both of us sitting in the chairs in front of my desk.

"This is where it all began," Lauren said, looking around the room.

I followed her gaze around the office and joined in her revelry, remembering the two strangers-soon-to-be-lovers who no longer resembled us in any substantially recognizable way. So very much had happened, so much loss, so much pain, yet here we were beyond all reasonable expectation, beyond all odds, beyond even belief, the two of us still here, different yet similar somehow to the lonely souls we had been.

"I feel so bad for those two young people," she said. "Wish I could go back and warn them."

I thought about what might be different if we could warn the earlier more innocent iterations of ourselves.

She noticed the magazine on my desk.

"You reading *Ring* again?" she asked.

I nodded.

I had always loved what took place in the squared circle of the boxing ring—had even fought in some amateur bouts and done well enough to make me dream at a little—but from the moment I lost my arm I had lost all interest in boxing.

Until now.

Being around the gym, seeing Freddy spar, smelling the leather and sweat, hearing the bell and the instructions from the corner . . . I was hooked again.

"How is it?" she asked.

I smiled at her, appreciative for her concern, but even more so for knowing to be.

"More of a bittersweet science now," I said.

She nodded. "Sorry. Can't help but think it's my fault."

"It's not."

"If I hadn't come through that door the first time . . . If we hadn't become . . . If I hadn't been stupid enough to try to end it . . ."

"I was just thinking about what you said about warning those two," I said. "The only thing I'd change is the pain you went through. I'd do whatever it took to take away your sickness and pain, but I wouldn't change anything. How could I? We wound up together. And as far as boxing or anything else, I'd give up anything for you, to be with you. Gladly. I'd give my other arm right now just for more time with you."

She reached over and took my remaining hand and held it, and we were quiet for a long moment.

Eventually, Miki appeared in the doorway.

She was pale, the lines of her face creases of discomfort.

"Are you okay?" I asked.

Lauren stood and walked over to her. "I want you to lie down for a while," she said. "Here, you can use Ray's old office."

They disappeared from view but I could still hear them. Lauren was saying, "Did you take the aspirin?"

"Just like Lady Boss Lauren say."

"Okay, try to sleep for a while."

When Lauren reappeared, I said, "Is she okay?"

"She's fine. Got a visitor today. Just needs to rest for a little while."

"A visitor?"

"Her monthly one."

"Oh."

She eased back down in the chair beside me, her slow movements revealing how she was really feeling.

Taking my hand again, picking up right where we had left off, she said, "I'm not doing enough . . . for others I mean. Staying with Gladys the little that I do is just . . . it's not enough."

I didn't say anything. Just waited. She'd get to what she wanted to say when she was ready.

"I know I'm limited in what I can do. I'm no Rosie."

She was referring to Rosie the Riveter, the tireless assembly line–working woman popularized a year or so back in the song by Redd Evans and John Jacob Loeb and in the Norman Rockwell painting on the cover of the *Saturday Evening Post* last Memorial Day.

"I'm still so weak," she continued, "and I don't know how much time I have left, but . . . when I'm not with you—which I want to be as much as possible—I don't want to just be sitting around waiting to die."

I adored so very many things about Lauren, but this, her generosity and graciousness, her gratitude and desire to give back, was near the top of the list.

"If it's okay with you . . ." she began, "I'd like to volunteer at the USO."

The USO, or United Service Organization, was formed in 1941 by several civilian groups including the Salvation Army, the YMCA, and the National Jewish Welfare Board, as a home away from home to boost morale and provide recreational services for uniformed servicemen. My understanding was the private organization was partnering with the government—in particular the Department of Defense. The government was providing the buildings and the organization raising funds to staff and operate them, fulfilling the mission of bolstering morale for the military by providing on-leave recreation for uniformed personnel.

After the first USO Club was established in Louisiana in 1941, they began popping up all over the world, something like two a day by now, offering our troops a place to congregate, to dance, to listen to music, to be social, to relax, to have a cup of coffee and an egg, to write a letter home, to enjoy the attentions of a pretty girl.

Our local USO club was located at the end of Harrison Avenue right on the bay.

"What would you do?" I asked.

"I'd be a junior hostess."

I knew that was what she was going to say but I was still unprepared for how it would make me feel.

Junior hostesses were the young women whose job it was to socialize, comfort, entertain, hang out with, dance with, and boost the morale of the servicemen making the USO their home away from home. It was an honorable job that attempted to keep our boys out of bars and brothels, but it was also fraught with many perils and pitfalls, an emotional minefield for the young serviceman, perhaps the young hostess, and certainly for the young hostess's—what? What was I to Lauren? I wasn't her husband, but I was far more than a boyfriend. That I was even asking demonstrated the difficulties of her doing this.

I felt completely confident in us, had complete faith in her, but that was a relatively recent phenomenon. For much of our relationship I had suffered bouts of jealousy, of obsession and suspicion, particularly following our first breakup and the devastating rejection I experienced because of it.

How would I handle her role as companion to lonely, scared, homesick young men in a uniform I would never get to wear?

"It's just the senior hostesses are supposed to be at least thirty-five," she said.

Theoretically, senior hostesses played the role of mother, while the junior hostesses were meant to be more like sisters, neighbor girls-next-door, and friends.

"If you'd rather me not, I'll find another way to serve," she said. "I just thought it would be a good fit given my physical limitations and lack of energy."

"I'm so . . ." I began. "You're such an amazing person. Just promise me you won't overdo it. Please take care of yourself."

"I will. I promise. For you even more than me. Really? You're sure you don't mind?"

"You'll be so good at it," I said, avoiding her question. "Do so much good for those who need it most, who themselves are doing so much good. I'm . . . just so proud of you. You inspire me. Wish I could do more."

Chapter 10

I walked Lauren down the stairs toward the sidewalk and Harrison Avenue below, feeling as if my center had caved in a bit, but when we emerged, another more urgent sensation replaced it.

Parked just a few spots down from us was the vehicle I equated with threat as much as any cop car—a six-passenger Presidential Delux–style Land Cruiser with a black roof, the extremely rare whitewall tires, and a back glass with ventilating wings.

It belonged to Miki's uncle, the man who had promised to kill me the next time he saw me if I didn't produce Miki for him.

Lauren followed my gaze over to the car.

"Is that . . ."

As usual, wartime Harrison was busy, steady traffic on the street, the sidewalks bustling with people—shoppers, couples, mothers with strollers, businessmen, and military personnel in uniform.

From out of the crowd all around us a young Japanese man wearing a hat and large, dark sunglasses to help hide his identity stepped up behind Lauren, wrapping his right arm around her waist while pointing a small revolver into her side with his left. His suit coat hid most of his hand and the gun in it.

He pulled her over toward our building, pressing his back to the door of our walkup.

I followed.

As I did, a broad middle-aged Japanese man with dense black hair and thick orangish skin, also mostly hidden beneath a hat and behind dark glasses, stepped up behind me and jammed a gun of his own into my back. He was wearing the same three-button tan Glen Plaid sports coat and solid medium brown wool slacks with pleats and cuffs as before, the same hand-painted tie and brown-and-tan wingtips.

He was Miki's uncle here to make good on his promise.

Lauren and I were face to face, pressed into one another, sandwiched together by the two armed men.

"I love you," I said.

Her eyes locked onto mine and I saw something in them, a calmness and fearlessness that made me admire and appreciate her all the more.

"Borrowed time," she said. "Get the most out of every moment—even these."

I nodded.

"You ah find ah niece?" he asked.

"You're gonna do this here?" I asked. "In front of all these people?"

"You ah find her ah or no?"

"Things have changed," I said.

When he had first approached me, I was wanted for murder, operating in the shadows like him and his small community of fugitives who had escaped from Manzanar, a relocation camp for citizens of Japanese descent situated on the edge of the desert along the eastern slope of the Sierra Nevada.

Because I couldn't go to the police, they had turned to me for help. Because I was isolated and wounded and didn't want to stop my search for those responsible for what had happened to Lauren and my old partner Pete, I had not only worked for them but allowed them to bully me a bit—something I was no longer prepared to do.

"How ah so?" he said.

"You and I have even less in common now."

"You ah explain. Now."

"I'm no longer sideways with the cops. You still are."

"This ah change ah nothing for ah you," he said. "You ah die just as ah easy. Girl too."

"Good point," I said. "Okay. I found her, yes. I haven't been able to get her, but I can. I just need a little longer."

"You ah bring her to ah beach tonight. Same ah spot. Eight ah clock. Or we ah kill you. And girl."

"I'll be there."

"We ah take girl make ah sure you ah are."

I shook my head. "No. I'll be there. I found her before. I'll find her again. I'll be there tonight. Like I said. You have my word. I've never given you a reason to doubt that I do what I say I will."

"We ah still ah take girl. Just ah safe ah side."

I shook my head again. "No," I said again. "That's not acceptable. You walk away now and I meet you tonight or we do this in the street right now. You get caught. Go to jail. Never see your niece again. Up to you?"

He didn't say anything, just increased the pressure of the barrel in the small of my back.

"All I have to do is yell Jap right now," I said, "and you're captured and sent back to the internment camp."

"Unless ah I ah shoot you."

"Then you go to jail or get ah killed yourself. Up to you. But you're not leaving here with my . . . with Mrs. Lewis."

"Okay ah cowboy. See you tonight at ah eight."

With that they vanished back into the crowd, the car starting the moment they did, backing out as soon as the two men were back inside, easing into the stream of traffic and disappearing down the way.

Lauren and I leaned into an intense embrace.

"You okay?" I asked.

She nodded, her weak head rising and falling slowly beneath my chin.

"Sorry about that."

"I'm just glad Judy got her period today."

After making sure Lauren was okay and tucking her and Miki into a room at the Dixie Sherman under a different name, I drove back to my office to meet Clip to make a plan.

On the way, I stopped by the Lighthouse Café.

I couldn't help myself.

Located on the lower end of Harrison Avenue, not far from the USO, the Lighthouse looked like a large milk bottle.

It was just after lunch and the crowd was gone. The tables, in need of bussing, were littered with dirty dishes—most of those empty, with only smears of catsup and gravy remaining, others with partially eaten meals.

The place looked suddenly and abruptly abandoned.

Nell, in her pressed waitress uniform and soiled apron, was standing near the back, a plate of food in her hand.

She was an extremely thin middle-aged woman with shortish curly hair and long, bony fingers.

She smiled and waved and I walked over toward her.

"You got a minute?" I asked.

"Long as you don't mind me eating," she said. "I'm starvin'."

We sat at one of the few clean tables toward the back and she began attacking wartime food as if it tasted better than it looked, which, having eaten here often, I knew did not.

"Evidently your thinness is not from lack of appetite or eating," I said.

She smiled.

"What can you tell me about the junior hostesses at the USO?" I asked.

I had so much I needed to be doing, so many things to figure out and plan, but this was what I'd be thinking about while trying to do all of them if I didn't deal with it now.

I knew Nell had volunteered at the USO as a senior hostess. I knew she would shoot straight with me. I knew she would know what she was talking about.

"They're good girls," she said. "Doing good work. Really providing a great service."

She paused for a moment to take another big bite of her food, then continued.

"Those girls are probably doing more for the morale of our boys than anyone else in the country."

"What kind of training do they receive?"

"None really. Some take a charm school class, but . . ."

"Are they all single?"

"Most, but not all. More of the senior hostesses are married than the juniors, but there's a fair number of them that are too."

"Why do most of them do it?"

She shrugged her thin, skeletal shoulder. "I'm sure

I can't say. To serve their country, to help us beat the Japs and the Nazis—"

"Are most wanting to meet servicemen? Looking for a husband?"

"Most?" she asked, her gaunt face scrunching up in consideration of the question. "Maybe. Probably."

"Are they allowed to date?" I said. "To see the servicemen outside of the club?"

"It's discouraged, but can hardly be stopped. You know? Why all the questions, fella? This for a case? Somethin' happen to one of the girls?"

"Just background."

"They're good girls," she said. "They keep these boys away from bottles and loose broads and help keep their spirits up. Do things get out of hand sometimes? Sure. Do lonely boys take things to mean things they don't? Sure. Are some of the girls trying to find a brave soldier husband? Of course. But is it a great program worth having? Absolutely."

Chapter 12

When Clip walked into my office he tossed a copy of the *News Herald* onto my desk.

"You see dis shit?" he said. "Like the nigger tryin' to git hisself killed."

An article about the upcoming fight quoted Freddy making a variety of inflammatory statements about the country, the culture, the war, and the oppressive power structure—by which he meant white people without saying it.

I nodded.

"He ain't wrong," Clip said.

"No, he's not."

"But gotdamn, he ain't got to say it like that and in there."

"Maybe he does," I said. "Maybe somebody does."

He shrugged. "Maybe so. Well, enough about loudmouth niggers. Let's rap about what to do about these damn Japs."

Before I could respond, I heard the door downstairs open and someone climbing the stairs.

I stood and walked out, Clip joining me, his gun

drawn.

When we reached the stairs and looked down we saw Saul and Freddy Freeman walking up.

"Who the hell you expecting?" Saul asked.

"Or dis how you greet every client?" Freddy said.

"Nah," Clip said, "just the dumbass niggers that run they mouth in the papers."

"Okay if we come up?" Saul asked.

From up above him, I could see that he had even less wispy white hair than I realized, and watching him climb the steps showed he was weaker and more feeble than projected by his posture and bearing.

"Sure," I said.

A few minutes later, the four of us were in my office—Freddy and Saul in my client chairs, me behind my desk, Clip partially propped up against a filing cabinet in the corner to my left.

"What's with the muggin' in the mornin' paper?" Clip asked.

"Somebody gotta say it," Freddy said.

"That's what Jimmy said."

Freddy looked at me in surprise. "Oh, yeah? Now ain't that a kick."

"Why it gotta be you?" Clip said.

"Who else? I the one they listenin' to right now. Sorta like nigger of the month. You mights be happy bein' a house nigger, but—"

"I seem like a house nigger to you?"

"The reason we're here," Saul said, "is to apologize for how the first meeting went, and to hire you to find out who's threatenin' Freddy and to protect him while you do."

I didn't say anything and we waited.

And waited.

After a few moments of awkward silence, Clip and I smiled at each other.

"Oh," Clip said, "that the apology?"

"Only one y'alls likely to get from me," Freddy said.

"It was my fault," Saul said. "I shoulda spoken to everyone ahead of time so we all knew what to expect and—"

"Wasn't your fault, Saul," Clip said. "It just your house nigger got no manners."

Freddy started to say something, but instead stood up and walked out without a word.

"I was really hoping we could figure this out," Saul said. "He's in real danger—more now after the article this morning. I know he's . . . a . . . that he's challenging, but he's sincere in what he's saying. He's not just boxing. He really is using his moment to . . . to try and—"

From down on the street shots were fired.

Glass shattered. Women screamed. Horns honked. Tires screeched. And a loud thud was heard in the stairwell.

We jumped up and ran toward the stairs—Clip out in front, gun drawn, me not far behind, Saul quite a few steps farther back.

"You hit?" Clip yelled.

"Nah. They missed me."

"Go upstairs with Saul," Clip said, passing Freddy and continuing through the shattered glass door out onto the sidewalk.

I followed him.

Outside, people were still scattered in every direction, ducking for cover, consoling one another.

"Which way?" Clip yelled. "Which way?"

No one seemed to know.

We looked around, but saw no shooters, saw no one reacting to shooters attempting to make an escape.

We searched the crowd for a few minutes, running toward the Ritz Theater and the Tennessee House, then back toward the drugstore and the Marie Motel, but there were no signs of any shooters anywhere, and though everyone seemed to have heard the shots, no one actually saw those responsible for them.

When we were back in my office with Saul and Freddy, I asked, "What'd you see?"

"Didn't see shit," Freddy said. "Heard the shots and screams, glass started shattering, and I dove back up the steps as far as I could."

"Did the shots come from a passing car or a gunman on the sidewalk?" Clip asked.

"Just tol' you. I didn't see."

"Okay," Clip said. "Well, good luck out there."

"Wait," Freddy said. "Look man, I'm sorry. All right? I wanna hire y'all. Should have before. Okay? I've got a big mouth."

"Big?" Clip asked. "Most oceans're smaller."

"You take the job or not?"

"Ain't takin' it 'cause it a job," Clip said. "The measly amount y'all ponyin' up ain't gonna pay no bills. Doin' it 'cause I want to, 'cause a loudmouth nigger oughta be able to fight without bein' threatened or killed, just like anybody else."

Chapter 13

"So you workin' the other side too," Clip said.

He was referring to Kay Hudson hiring me to find out what happened to Gentlemen Jeff Bennett.

I nodded.

"And dealin' with the threat from the Japs," he said.

I nodded again.

"Then we gonna need some help coverin' ol' Fast Mouth Freddy in there."

We were standing in the reception area not far from the staircase. Below us, cops milled about, asking questions, taking notes, waiting for Henry Folsom to arrive. Saul and Freddy were in my office, Saul comforting and reassuring Freddy, Freddy reevaluating his life.

"We can't afford anyone," I said.

He had no idea just how bad things were. Kay Hudson's small retainer would pay for the room at the Cove and for us to eat for maybe a week, but that's about all it would do. I was still three months behind on the rent here at our offices and the landlord was threatening to kick us out if I didn't catch it up soon.

"I'a see what I can do," he said. "Maybe cash in a

marker I been holdin' or make some sorta side deal, you know, pay a brother in a different way."

"Even if you can, it's gonna have to be mostly us."

He nodded. "Know," he said. "It help we didn't have the Jap distraction tonight."

"Yes, it would."

"Got any thoughts on how to do that exactly?" he asked.

"I do," I said, "and I don't like them. Don't like them at all."

"Don't let your conscience get in the way of us protectin' that good girl," he said. "She been through enough."

No one knew what she had been through like I did. I had seen it firsthand the night I found her. No one wanted to take care of her more than I did—except maybe Clip now that he had fallen for her. But I couldn't get okay with the only way I could think of to deal with the threat to her.

"I'm tryin' not to," I said, "but . . . how can I send innocent people back to prison?"

The internment camps were wrong. The small community hiding at the beach who had escaped one of them should not have to go back. Their only crime was being Japanese.

"*Innocent*?" he said. "Man's a thug."

"Sure," I said, "but what about the others? It's an all-or-nothing deal."

"You talkin' about gettin' 'em sent back to a camp," he said.

I nodded. "And I don't know if Miki would even be okay with that, with setting up her family, her mother."

"She is," he said. "But aksk her yourself."

"Camps don't bother you?" I asked.

"'Course they do. Lot a shit bother me. Imprison a man for the color of his skin. Do shit to all because of the actions of a few."

"Which is what we'd be doing," I said.

He started to say something, then stopped, then said, "Gotdamn but you can complicate some shit."

"Yeah," I said, "the world is simple and I keep complicating it."

"I gonna uncomplicate it for you. We can turn 'em in or I can shoot 'em."

While Clip kept watch over Freddy as he sparred at Bay High, I drove over to the Dixie Sherman to talk to Lauren and Miki.

Though it was all about Miki and involved her family, I wanted Lauren's thoughts on what I was proposing.

The only high-rise in town, the Dixie Sherman Hotel sat at the corner of Jenks Avenue and Fifth Street. Built in 1925 by W. C. Sherman, it had one hundred and one rooms, each with a bathroom and a telephone for only three bucks.

It wasn't until I was stepping out of the elevator that I realized the significance of the floor, and I paused for a moment to glance over at the spot where I had shot Stanley Somerset, and once again I missed Ray Parker and our secretary July.

Inside the room, I hugged Lauren and shared with her and Miki what I was planning.

"I just can't think of another solution," I said.

"They would all go back to camp?" Miki said.

"They would."

"Jimmy-san do this for me?"

"I would."

"No one get hurt?"

"I can't guarantee that," I said. "If your uncle or his boys resist . . . then . . . And if there're shots fired . . . anyone can get shot."

Miki seemed to think about it.

I looked at Lauren. "What do you think?"

"You know what I think. The camps are evil. Sending them back there is evil, but given the circumstances—them wanting to enslave Miki, to make her a . . . what I almost was—it's the lesser of two evils."

"Miki?" I said.

She frowned, twisted her lips, and shook her head. "Miki go back. Cannot risk Mama-san life."

Lauren nodded. "Okay. But you're not going back. Soldier will figure something else out."

"I will?"

"Sure you will, fella," she said. "It's what you do. Besides, you've got" —she glanced at the watch on her slender wrist— "nearly five hours to do it."

Chapter 14

When I got back down to the lobby, I asked Francis Stevens, the young redheaded bellboy, if I might have a word—and told him if he tossed a few back my way there'd be a buck in it for him.

According to Kay Hudson, the Dixie Sherman had been the last place Jeff and Rebecca Bennett was seen.

"I understand Jeff Bennett and his wife had a room here a few days back?"

"No, sir. No wife. Just Gentleman Jeff."

He jumped into a boxing stance and began to jab at the air.

Francis Stevens was too young to be a bellhop and looked it. The war had caused a shortage of young men—something the enterprising young Francis took advantage of. With his red hair showing beneath is cap, the boyishness of his pale, freckled face, his diminutive stature, and the way the small gray uniform swallowed him up, he looked like a kid playing bellhop in a comedy picture more than an actual bellboy.

"He was here alone?" I said.

"No, sir. I didn't say that, now did I?"

If this was a simple case of Jeff not being so gentlemanly and stepping out on Rebecca, it would practically solve itself.

"He had a different dame with him?" I said.

"No, sir. Nothin' like that. His manager maybe. I don't know for sure. Someone said it was his sparring partner."

"What happened?"

"Whatta you mean?"

"Anything eventful happen while he was staying here? Anything suspicious?"

"No, sir. I don't think he ever came out of his room until . . ."

"Until what?"

"Well I was gonna say until he checked out, but he never did. He just vanished. One minute he was here, the next he was not. And nobody saw him leave. Nobody saw nothin'."

"How long was he here?"

"Hard to say since we don't know exactly when he left, but I'd say somewhere in the neighborhood of three days?"

"How'd you know he was gone?"

"Girl went in to clean the room."

"So he took his stuff?"

"No—well, not everything. That's what was strange. She thought he had, but she found some stuff hidden when she was cleaning the room. You ask me, I say it proves he was taken against his will. He's not the sort likely to forget anything—'specially somethin' important enough to hide. And you'll never convince me Gentleman Jeff Bennett would ever skip out on a bill. Not in a million years."

"What did she find?" I asked. "Where is it now?"

"I don't know what all. I've just heard a word or two here and there. Some papers or somethin', a book or journal or . . . maybe some photographs."

"Where's the stuff now?"

"She turned it over to the manager and he turned it over to the cops."

Chapter 15

"Miki won't go for the plan," I said.

Clip and I were standing in the corner of the Bay High gym, watching as Freddy added serious bodily injury to the insult of being a sparring partner.

As usual, there were no reporters in the gym. The only access the press had to Freddy was following his workout when for a brief period they were allowed in to pepper the obnoxious, opinionated boxer with a total of two questions each.

"Not sure she got a choice," he said.

"Says she's goin' back."

"She absolutely got no choice about that."

"Doesn't want to take the risk of anyone getting hurt—mostly her mom."

He shook his head. "I'a protect her fuckin' mama-san. She ain't goin' back to that shit."

"Lauren told us to come up with a different plan."

"Us?"

"Well, you, but I figured I'd try to help."

He smiled his big, brilliant smile. "You come up with anything yet?"

"Maybe. Just now on the drive over here, but it's pretty damn thin."

"Let's hear it."

"We don't show tonight."

"Genius," he said.

"They come after us. But they won't send Miki's mom. It will be the old man and his gun boys. We have them picked up."

"'Less they shoot us first."

"It's not a perfect plan," I said.

"Big of you to admit."

I smiled.

"So we risk our lives and that of civilians instead of Bunko Matsumoto," he said.

"Would you rather risk your mother-in-law?"

He didn't respond, but I saw the twitch of something resembling the start of a smile on his large lips.

"My biggest concern," I said, "and I have many . . . But the biggest, and it was the same with the other plan too, is that once they're captured—"

"*If* they captured."

"If they're actually captured," I amended, "that they'll just turn Miki in."

He nodded. "Be better we just shoot 'em."

"*Jimmy*?" Folsom said when I walked into his office. "I'm surprised to see you here."

I nodded.

"Come on. Have a seat."

I did.

"I know I can't keep apologizing every time I see

you, but . . . I am so very sorry for what I let myself get sucked into, for looking the other way, for . . . for what it could've cost you."

I didn't say anything and we sat in silence for a few moments.

Things would never be the same between us again. He had betrayed me in the worst possible way—the way only an intimate father figure could, but his remorse made what I was here to ask for much easier.

"For what it's worth," he said, "I really did believe you'd figure a way out of all of it. I knew you and Clip could handle it."

My face must have revealed my skepticism.

"I honestly did," he said. "I'm not just saying that. And I was right."

"The things I was forced to do," I said. "What we were put through . . ."

"I really do feel terrible, son. And I'd like to spend the rest of my life making it up to you and winning back your trust."

"The latter will never happen," I said, "but the former . . . I'm actually here for a favor."

"Name it."

"Two favors, actually."

"Anything I can do," he said.

"Which you've proven is anything at all," I said.

"Jimmy," he said, "how about you not make this any harder than it has to be."

"I need help with a very delicate situation," I said. "It's gonna take some flexibility and finesse."

"Tell me."

I did.

When I finished he said, "Sounds straightforward enough. Capture the refugee thugs without anyone getting hurt and grant immunity to the girl."

I nodded.

"I can do that," he said. "I've got a new man I'll assign to it. Just joined the force. Reminds me a lot of you. He'll . . . he's perfect for the job."

"And Miki will be safe," I said.

"You've got to keep her hidden," he said. "There's only so much I can do. You can't parade her down Harrison Avenue for everyone to see, but I can make sure our guys don't come after her—no matter what the ones we take into custody say."

I nodded. "Thank you."

"That's nothin'. What else?"

"I want to know what you have on the Jeff Bennett disappearance and take a look at what he left in his room."

"We have nothing," he said. "Because there is nothing. He didn't disappear. He just went home without paying his bill—something his mother has assured me will be taken care of. As for what he left in the room, you can take it to him for us. Look at it all you like before you do."

Chapter 16

Driving back to the office to read over the materials Jeff Bennett left in his room, I spotted the two gargantuan twins walking down Harrison, their enormous upper bodies and huge heads rising above the throng of pedestrians moving like earth's landmass down the sidewalk.

I drove up a little past them, parked, and waited to see where they went.

In a few minutes they finally reached me, passing without ever looking my way, continuing on to Child's Drugs and Walgreen Agency on the corner, then crossing the street to the Marie Motel.

I got out of the car and followed them.

Buses to the beaches left from the Marie, charging fifteen cents one way or twenty cents round trip. One was loading at the moment and I lost sight of them as they disappeared behind the only thing around big enough to eclipse them.

When I rounded the bus, I saw the two giants talking to what appeared to be a midget, but was most likely an average man. After a few minutes of conversation, they crossed Harrison again, not stopping for traffic but forcing traffic to stop for them, and entered Child's, duckin' beneath the door as they did.

I waited a few minutes then crossed, but instead of going directly into Child's, I went next door to Christtos's 5 & 10, loitered outside, then stepped back over and entered Child's.

Inside I found the two behemoths at a booth with Miles Lydecker, a smallish middle-aged man in a black-market suit, eating a grilled cheese sandwich between sips of a brown cow—a foaming float of vanilla ice cream and root beer.

Miles Lydecker was the smallest, best-dressed, and most well-connected bookmaker in town.

Aha, I thought, then walked over to their table and said it out loud. "Aha."

The two big men looked surprised to see me, but Miles only looked mildly annoyed.

"Hiya Riley," he said. "Ain't seen you in a while. How's tricks? You don't look so good. Heard you lost the limb and left the force."

I nodded, but continued staring at the two goliaths across from him. "I just don't get it," I said.

"What don't you get?" Miles asked. "What?"

"How the booth, hell, the entire foundation of this joint isn't collapsing."

"American-made, baby," he said. "We do it better than anybody. Why we're gonna win the war."

I slid into the booth beside him.

He didn't move much, but he was small enough so that even though he was in the middle of the seat, there was still room for me.

"Riley, I'm eating and havin' a meeting with my

associates. I ain't got time for—"

"He was with the jig who showed up at the gym," the man across from me said.

"I've been hired to protect Freddy Freeman," I said.

They all laughed a little at that.

"Always with the jokes," Miles said.

"Why'd you send the brothers elephantine around to lean on him?" I asked.

"A, I ain't sayin' I did, but B, if I did, it would have nothin' whatsoever to do with you."

"Why don't you want him fighting?"

"I do," he said. "I want nothin' more."

"Then why threaten him? Why say you're goin' to kill him?"

He looked at his two associates. "What's this? Did you threaten to kill him?"

They both shook their heads. "No, sir," the one across from me said. "Was just tellin' him what you told us to when this guy shows up and . . ."

"We have not threatened to kill anyone," Miles said. "It's bad for business."

"Why threaten to break his hand so he can't box if you want nothin' more than for him to fight?" I said. "Seems a contradiction."

"Reminding him he can't fight with a broken hand is not the same as breaking it. That is not to say that I would not break it if I had to, but Freddy is an, ah, associate of mine, and I wish him nothing but the best. Now, I know you're young and you look like you been through a war of your own, but you got a lot to learn, and you need to know a good deal more than you do before you *aba* up to the grownups table. Understand?"

I did, but I didn't tell him that.

"And one more thing," he said. "Call it a free tip from your Uncle Miles. The only person your client needs protecting from is himself."

Chapter 17

Walking back to my office from Child's, I noticed a tall, too-thin man with a subtle limp moving toward me.

His gate was slow and deliberate and somewhat self-conscious. He worked hard to conceal the limp, but there was only so much he could do.

It was obvious he was a cop.

Based on Henry Folsom's description of him, I'd say he was David Howell, the new cop who reminded Folsom of me—and who Folsom had assigned to help with my Japanese problem.

We met on the sidewalk in front of J.C. Penney's.

"Jimmy?" he asked.

I nodded and extended my left hand, which he took without awkwardness or hesitation.

My guess was he'd spent enough time around one-armed and injured men while recuperating from his own war wounds to be comfortable with loss of nearly every kind. I didn't know the story behind the limp and according to Folsom it wasn't something he ever spoke about.

"David Howell," he said. "Henry Folsom sent me over to talk to you."

"Howell," I said. "Any relation to Frank?"

Frank Howell had been the mayor before Harry Lewis.

"Distantly," he said.

"Small town," I said.

We stepped out of the middle of the sidewalk to the front of the building, pedestrians passing around us like river water flowing around the bases of cypress trees.

He glanced back down toward my office. "German's attack your office?"

I smiled. "For all I know."

"Well, looks like whoever it was was committed."

"Germans are certainly that."

"But I guess we're meant to be talkin' about Japs not Germans, right?"

I nodded.

Through the windows behind us, customers, mostly women, were making purchases from Penney's through a cable pulley system that transported payment from customers at various locations throughout the sales floor to the office in the back.

"What'd he tell you?" I asked.

"To do whatever I could to help you," he said. "To do it with discretion and make sure no one gets hurt. Didn't give me a lot of details."

I took care of that, filling him in on everything he needed to know.

"So," he said, "you don't show at eight tonight, they come after you, we grab 'em."

"*Before* they shoot me," I said.

"Before they shoot you," he said, nodding. "That's right."

David Howell had a relaxed ease about him that was appealing. He was still and quiet—economical with his words and actions, and self-contained the way most men who did what we did were. He seemed somewhat scathed, perhaps even shell-shocked, but self-assured nonetheless.

"I take it Folsom feels like he owes you."

I didn't say anything, just waited.

"He tells me to help you, you can count on my help—and after hearing your story . . . I want to help. Hell, it's why I'm a cop."

I nodded.

"But . . . you need to know . . . I won't do anything illegal. I enforce the law. I catch those who break it. I don't break it myself—or even bend it. Not even in the pursuit of criminals. Understand?"

I nodded.

"Too many good men dying for what's right. I won't dishonor them. I won't dishonor my department or myself."

"If that's true, and I hope it is," I said, "it'll be a welcomed surprise."

Back in my office, I took a quick look at Jeff Bennett's papers.

There was much in them that didn't make sense—documents and notes I couldn't decipher.

From what I could gather based on the little I could understand, he was working on a story about war profiteering and the thriving black market in our area.

I saw a few names I recognized—including that of Lee Perkins, who until his recent demise had ruled all things black market in the region from his lair in the Floridan Hotel in Tallahassee.

Perkins's name had a line through it. Above it was scribbled: *Who takes over now that he's dead?*

I had wondered that myself. I hadn't lost any sleep over it or anything, but I had been curious as to whether another predator had already taken his place, stepping into the vacant position my actions had created.

Would he, like so many other dictators, crime bosses, and kingpins, be replaced with someone or some*ones* worse? Had my dishonorable actions made the world better—even a bit, even marginally—or had they led to something that was, like the actions themselves, degrading and despicable?

My plan had been to study the papers a bit and then take them to Jeff, but as I left for his mother's place in the Cove where he was said to be, his things were left behind once again—this time hidden beneath some boxing magazines in a bottom drawer of my desk.

Lady Bird Bennett, Jeff's mother and the woman many claimed was the mother of Panama City, lived in a Spanish-style home only slightly smaller than a football stadium on Bunker's Cove overlooking the bay.

The house, which was beautiful, would have looked more at home in St. Augustine than Panama City—and, in fact, it had been designed and built by one of the leading architects who brought the Spanish Colonial Revival style to St. Augustine, Tampa, and Miami.

Large enough to be a hotel instead of a house, the enormous structure was all pristine white smooth plaster walls and chimneys, low-pitched clay tile roofs, small second- and third-floor balconies, double-hung windows with canvas awnings, terra-cotta ornaments, and decorative iron trim.

By the time I had walked up the brick drive, Lady Bird Bennett was waiting for me in between the enormous wooden doors of the open entryway.

She was as vibrant as any sixty-year-old woman I had ever encountered—tall, but not too, solid, but trim, erect with perfect posture, but not rigid.

Beneath coarse, stylishly long gray hair, her big blue eyes were bright and penetrating.

She extended her left hand even before I did and we shook like men, her grip firm, strong, but not in the overly so manner of some men trying to signify something from the jump.

"Good of you to come," she said, though I had requested the meeting.

"Thanks for seeing me."

"It's only a little nippy," she said. "If it's agreeable with you, I thought we might sit out here and enjoy the crisp air."

"Sure," I said, wondering if it were just a way to keep the cheap detective out of the nice house and off the expensive furniture.

She indicated a set of wooden chairs to her right and we walked over and sat down in them. Between them was a table with a tray of what looked to me like an English tea and biscuits—something as uncommon in the deep South as Spanish Colonial Revival mansions and boxing war correspondents.

"I much prefer tea to coffee," she said. "Hope that's okay by you."

"Sure. Tea is fine."

"I don't take mine with sugar, but I'm sure I could find some on the premises if you required it."

"Not at all," I said.

"I put tupelo honey in mine," she said.

"Sounds good," I said, and it was.

"Now," she said, "I don't mean to be indelicate, but it's a small town and one hears things."

"From what I hear, it's your town and you hear

everything."

She smiled at that, seeming to find my comment more ingratiating than insulting.

"You're the hero cop that lost his arm saving that woman and her child," she said. "The one who ran off with Harry Lewis's wife and had some trouble. Everyone thought both of you were dead, then you showed up and were suspected of all manner of . . . of murder and various crimes, then that somehow blew over. Now I hear Mrs. Lewis is back from the grave too, but Harry's no longer with us. You worked with the former Pinkerton . . . What was his name? Parker. He too is no longer among the quick. And as I understand it, though it seems quite incredible, you've taken over his agency and are a private detective."

"Why do you find that incredible?" I asked.

"Does our little town really need a private detective? Are we big enough? Are we crime-ridden enough to need the services of a—"

"Well, Mrs. Bennett—"

"Call me Birdie," she said. "Mrs. Bennett will always be my late husband's mother."

"—take for instance your son dropping out of the bout and going missing," I said. "Someone's got to look into that."

"But he's merely believed to be missing," she said.

"Either way."

"And the police?"

"There's a lot they don't have time for," I said. "Or are uninterested in pursuing past a certain point."

"I see. Very interesting. I find it all so fascinating. I really do. I find you fascinating, Mr. Riley."

"Jimmy, please," I said. "Mr. Riley will always be my

late father."

She smiled and something mischievous danced in her eyes and twitched at the corners of her lips.

Down the driveway, past landscaped beds and small gardens, in the opposite direction from the one I had entered and parked, a hundred feet or so from the house, a man in a white uniform complete with hat was cleaning a car in front of a three-car garage that matched the house.

The car was a '42 black Nash Ambassador with plenty of chrome—including a wraparound grille, above which were the three signature horizontal bars, and matching side trim. Even in the dull daylight, the car gleamed as if beneath perfect summer sunlight.

"So, if I could just speak with your son, Mrs. . . . Birdie, I can get all this cleared up and be out of your way and get back to my other cases."

"You actually have other cases?"

"I do."

"Really? That's . . . Can one actually make a living being a private eye in Panama City?"

"The verdict is still out on that one," I said.

"I just can't imagine," she said. "I really can't."

"The thing you have to remember, Mrs. . . . Birdie . . . is people define making a living very differently. Take you and me for instance . . ."

She smiled again. "Well, you've won me over, Mr. . . . Jimmy. If I'm ever in need of the services of a shamus, you're who I'm calling."

"That's good of you," I said. "Now about your son."

"Yes," she said, "down to business. I need to know I can trust your discretion."

"You can," I said.

"But—"

"What have you heard about the Callahan case?" I asked.

The Callahans were another wealthy family living in the Cove.

"Why nothing," she said.

"Exactly."

She smiled again—the same smart, self-amused smile.

"I couldn't do what I do," I said, "couldn't keep doing it, if I was a blabber mouth. Telling me something is like telling it to your priest."

"Mr. . . . Jimmy, I'm Protestant, as I'm sure you know."

"It was just an analogy."

"The thing is, my son is sick, and I want to keep that out of the papers and out of the wagging tongues of the silly women who make up the gossip guild of the grapevine of our small community."

"What kind of sick?" I asked.

"What do you mean?"

"What's wrong with him?"

"It's not just one thing," she said. "It's one cause—the war, the things he's been through over there—but it's affecting him in a variety of ways. He's mentally exhausted. He's physically frail."

"May I speak with him?" I asked. "I'll be brief."

"He needs to rest, to be away from all stress and pressure and even activity for a while. Then he'll be back, then he'll be right as rain again."

"I won't upset him," I said. "I won't tire him. I'll just—"

"He's not here or I'd let you," she said. "I've arranged for special treatment for him in a relaxing setting. Do you know why? Do you know what his most important job is, Mr. Riley? It's not reporting and it's certainly not boxing. It's having an heir, making sure the future of our family and all we do is secure."

"Where is he? Could I visit him there?"

"I'm sorry," she said. "It's just not possible. I wish it were, but . . . I'd be happy to set up a time for you to come see him once he's home."

"When will that be?"

"I'm not sure. It will depend on how he responds to the treatment, how much time he needs to heal and . . . I just don't know. But given the good stock he comes from, I can't imagine it will take long."

"Is Mrs. Bennett with him?"

"Oh, you mean Rebecca? I thought she was who hired you."

I shook my head.

"Then I don't know where she is. I'm afraid part of what's going on are some marital difficulties. *Oh*, of course. I know who hired you—it's that correspondent. What's-her-name Hudson."

"I can't say," I said. "I never reveal anything about a client."

"Then it sounds like I need to be one of your clients," she said. "You've gotten me to reveal all sorts of things I didn't intend to today. Tell you what, let me hire you to find Rebecca. Can't very well have an heir without getting these two back together. How does a five-hundred-dollar retainer sound?"

Like a bribe, I thought but didn't say to her.

"And Jimmy . . . you should know . . . Miss Hudson's intentions toward my son are not honorable. Don't let her manipulate you. Any marital issues brought on by the stress and trauma of the war pale by comparison to the assault of Kay Home-wrecker Hudson. Ask around. She has a reputation."

Chapter 19

"Okay," I said, "we have a new plan."

I was back in Lauren and Miki's room in the Dixie Sherman.

Lauren seemed weaker and more tired than before, Miki bored, restless.

"We don't show tonight," I said. "Your uncle and his gunsels come after me. The cops arrest them. Leaves your mom out of it. No one gets hurt—except maybe one of your uncle's little gun boys."

Miki was nodding. "Much better plan, Soldier Boss Man."

Lauren said, "But won't they just turn on Miki? All they have to do is tell the—"

"Folsom gave me his word they wouldn't come after her."

"What? You told him? You trust him again?"

"No, but I do believe him—on this."

She shook her head and frowned. "I hope you're right. Think about the consequences to Miki if you're not."

"I have. I am. Not thinking of much else at the moment."

Eight o'clock came and went.

I didn't show. I had broken my word again—something I was doing with far too much regularity these days.

Clip, David Howell, and I were in my office.

We were waiting.

One of Clip's cousins, a big, bad middle-aged man who was good with a gun and better with a knife, was taking a shift with Freddy tonight. The man's name was Franklin. He had worked as a bouncer at the only black club in town and could handle himself just fine.

I didn't have any such cousins, so a retired cop who was only okay with a gun and didn't own a knife was posted near the door to Lauren and Miki's room at the Dixie.

"Where you from?" Clip asked David.

"Carrabelle."

"Best seafood I ever had was in Carrabelle. Best few other things too."

David smiled. "A woman," he said. "Man says somethin' that way, he can only be talking about a woman."

"Not just any woman," Clip said.

"The best woman," David said.

"She ain't the best at everything, but damn if she ain't the very best at a few things."

"Is your experience of Carrabelle women similar?" I asked David.

He shook his head. "None I ever knew were the best at anything. Hell, I can't say they were particularly good at anything."

"Carrabelle where you got that little hitch in your

giddyup?" Clip asked.

David shook his head, but didn't say anything.

"Guess that happen when you's off seein' the world with your uncle," Clip added.

David gave the slightest of nods.

We all fell silent for a while.

Eventually Clip said, "Be hell of a lot easier they come tonight when we expectin' them. Get it over with."

"Would," I said.

"But it ain't lookin' all that good for that, is it?"

"No, it's not," I said.

"Now no matter what else we doin', we got to keep an eye out for them."

"Yes, we do."

"You got any idea how hard that shit is for a nigger with only one eye?"

"I'm not goin' anywhere," David said. "I'll be around when they do come. We'll get them."

Ultimately it didn't matter that they didn't show, or that everything else we were doing would be made more difficult while we waited for them to make their move, or that the gunshot wound in my gut hurt like hell, or that I was raw-boned and marrow-weary—because later that night I got to crawl into a soft, warm bed beside Lauren Lewis. Next to that, nothing mattered. Nothing in the world.

"Hey," she whispered, turning toward me, pressing her body and lips to mine. "What happened?"

I had joined her in the room at the Dixie Sherman. Miki was asleep in the bed next to ours, her rhythmic breathing nearly but not quite a snore.

"They didn't show."

"What's that mean?"

"That Miki's uncle is thinking strategically instead of emotionally, that this could go on a while, that he may prove to be a far more formidable foe than I thought."

"How are you?" she asked.

"I'm the happiest man in the world," I said. "How are you feeling?"

"Just tired, but happy too. So happy."

"Get some sleep," I said.

"I don't want to sleep," she said. "Don't want to do anything but be with you—to hold each other and talk all night. Well, what there is left of it."

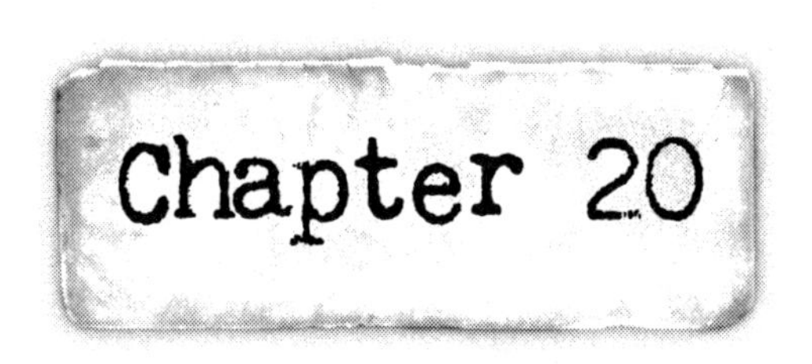

Chapter 20

I felt like I had a big bulls-eye on my back, as if every move I made was being watched through the scope of a high-powered rifle.

It made me feel awkward, stiff, self-conscious.

Walking from my car to the Bay High gym, I actually scanned the area and looked over my shoulder several times.

The morning sun was high overhead, the day bright but cold, the biting wind causing the palm fronds to rub each other and clack together.

No one shot at me.

I made it to the door and walked inside.

Clip and Saul were sitting in the bleachers, watching as Freddy's sparring partner stalked him around the ring. He probably outweighed Freddy by eighty pounds or more, but he was slow, his movements lumbering, each punch preceded by a Western Union telegram announcing it was on its way.

"We need to talk," I said to Saul.

"Okay."

"Freddy too."

"He time it right," Clip said, "he could come over in between fat boy's punches. He'd never know he was gone."

When Saul stopped the action and called Freddy over, I thought the sparring partner was going to come over and hug him. Instead he remained over in the ring with Freddy's trainer, Gus, who immediately began coaching him on what he had been doing wrong.

"What?" Freddy said when he reached us, holding out his gloved hands in a way that conveyed both question and frustration.

"I solved the case," I said.

"You did?" Saul said. "Already?"

"The two big bastards who came in and threatened to break your hand," I said. "You know who they are and why they came."

Freddy didn't say anything.

I turned to Saul. "Do you?"

"Huh?"

"He knows them," I said. "Do you?"

"No. He does?" he said to me, then turning asked, "Freddy, you do? Who are they?"

"Doesn't matter," I said. "Who they are's not important. Who they work for is."

"Who?"

"Miles Lydecker."

"*The bookie*?" Saul said, his voice rising in volume and pitch.

He looked over at Freddy.

Freddy stared back defiantly.

"This true, Freddy?" he asked, but I could tell he knew it was.

"Is what true?" he said.

"How much you into him for?"

"How much what?"

Clip cleared his throat. "Answer a question with a question again and see if I don't knock you on your ass."

"I owe him some, yeah. So what?"

"How much?" Clip said.

"Five."

"Five hundred dollars?" Saul said.

"Five thousand."

"Fuck, Freddy," Clip said. "'Round here, nigger get killed over five dollars."

"He ain't wantin' to kill me."

"Thought that why you hired us," Clip said.

"Death threats ain't comin' from him. Got nothin' to do with him. They comin' from somebody else."

"The hell make you think that?"

"Miles want me fightin'," he said.

"So you can pay him back?" Saul said. "Do you know how many fights that would take?"

"He say I can pay him what I owe him with this one fight. Say all I gots to do is be beatin' the guy bad, then when he say to, go down and not get up."

"What the fuck?" Saul said. "We're doin' all this, working so hard, just for you to throw the fight?"

"No, sir. I'm not going to. Why you think he keep sendin' those big sons a bitches to threaten me?"

"Whatcha think?" Clip asked.

I shrugged. "Hard to protect a man from himself."

He nodded.

Freddy was working out with Gus, moving between

the speed and heavy bags so rhythmically as to be musical, the beat of his actions so distinct it was as if I could hear the song he was doing it to.

When we had started to leave, Saul had asked us to wait for a moment while he retrieved something from the locker room, which is what we were doing standing over near the exit talking now.

"Whatcha wanna do?" Clip said.

"It's your call."

"Know you gots enough to worry about without this shit. Japs alone are . . ."

I shook my head. "Only question is what you want to do," I said. "You say we're in, we're in. You say we walk, we walk."

"Can't believe the dumb motherfucker lied to me."

"People lie," I said. "People desperate enough to hire people like us lie a lot. First rule in the PI handbook—all clients lie."

"Why I just hearin' there a handbook?"

"You made it sound to him like we were still on the job," I said.

"But if there's no real threat—"

"The threats are real," Saul said.

He had just emerged from the locker room and was standing behind us holding a file folder.

He handed the folder to Clip instead of me—a show of respect that made me appreciate Saul Behr more than I thought possible.

Clip opened it and we both flipped through the death threat notes inside.

There were several. Letters cut out from various publications—mostly newspapers—pasted on pristine white typing paper. Each note was a variation on the same theme: Get the nigger to drop out of the fight or he dies.

"All of them have been addressed to me," Saul said, "left in various places."

"These ain't from Miles," Clip said.

"No," I said, "they're not."

"Guess we should find out who they *is* from," he said.

"Guess we should," I said.

Chapter 21

Kay Hudson was waiting for me when I got out of my car in front of my office.

She seemed to just want a brief chat on the sidewalk, but, target that I was, that wasn't something I could do.

Leading her up the stairs, she commented on the boarded-up door and bullet holes, and I told her what had happened.

"You're mixed up in some stuff, aren't you, fella?"

Our offices were empty and cold, and made me feel lonely. Made my various wounds ache even more too.

Inside my office, I placed the folder of death threats on my desk and we sat down.

"I just wanted a quick update," she said.

When I told her what Francis Stevens and Henry Folsom had said, she had nodded quietly, but her reaction to what Birdie said was quite different.

"She's lying," she said.

"About which part?" I asked.

"All of it, I'm sure," she said. "Everything that comes out of her mouth is a lie."

I didn't say anything, just waited.

"You don't believe me? You think because she has money and power she's honest?"

"Actually, those things bias me in the opposite direction."

"Well, good . . . because she's . . . a conniving, evil old . . . She's always tried to control her son—and until recently has succeeded. That's what's changed. That's why he's missing. Don't buy any bullshit about him convalescing somewhere. And acting as if she doesn't know where Rebecca is . . . Hiring you to find her—that's just her way of inserting her money and her will into the case. Think about it. Why wouldn't she tell you where he was?"

"I have," I said.

"Huh?"

"Thought about it."

"Oh. And?"

"I agree . . . her motives aren't what they seem."

"Well, that's a relief," she said. "For a minute there I thought—"

"But what about yours?"

"My . . ."

"Motives," I said. "Will you be more honest than she's being? Why hire me to find Jeff, Mrs. Hudson? You don't really expect me to believe you're just a concerned colleague."

"She called me a home wrecker, didn't she?"

I nodded.

"I have that reputation, I guess, but I'm not. My motives may be as mixed as the next fella's, but I assure you I'm not trying to take Jeff from Rebecca. And that's not what concerns Mrs. Bennett anyway. She doesn't care if Rebecca has him, so long as she does. That's what matters to her."

"An heir seemed pretty important to her too," I said. "But let's get back to you. You're not being completely honest with me."

"I am asking you, Mr. Riley, to find both Jeff and Rebecca. That's what I want you to do. Find them both—whether they're together or not. Would I be doing that if I wanted Jeff for myself?"

Before I could answer, the phone on July's desk rang.

"Excuse me a moment, please," I said.

I stood up slowly—more slowly than I intended.

"You okay?" she asked.

I nodded. "Still healing from . . . Move slower sometimes than others."

She stood. "Well, I won't keep you. Do call if you find out anything. Think about what I've said. And do be very careful where Lady Bird Bennett is concerned. You have no idea what she's capable of."

Nor she I, I thought but didn't say.

By the time I reached the phone, Kay Hudson was down the stairs and out the door.

Since I wasn't sure what to call the agency yet, I just said, "Hello."

"Jimmy?"

"Yeah."

"It's Francis."

"Hiya Francis. Got something good for me?"

"Gee, I wouldn't say that. No sir. It's not good at all. It's . . . it's more like—"

"Why not just tell me what it is?"

"Sure. Okay. Well, you know how I said Gentleman Jeff left without payin' his bill?"

"Yeah."

"Turns out that's not what happened at all. He didn't skip out on the bill. I should've known he wouldn't do that. A gentleman like him. I feel ashamed for even thinking it. Though, I guess now I wish that was what happened."

"Francis," I said.

"Yeah?"

"What is it? What'd you call to tell me?"

"Mr. Bennett didn't check out at all. He never even left the hotel at all. I mean, I guess he didn't. I guess he could have."

"Francis."

"He must've just moved or been moved," he said, "'cause he was just found murdered in a different room."

The moment I stepped off the elevator, Butch started shaking his head.

"No," he said, holding up his thick mitts. "No way. Turn right back around and go crawl back in whatever it was you crawled out of this morning."

He had stepped a few feet down the hallway toward me, leaving two uniformed officers near the doorway behind him.

Butch was a thick, dark bully with the look of the brawler about him—black, bushy hair, dark complexion, stubble, scar tissue around his eyes beneath unruly brows, and a nose that had been broken a few times.

He had become my ex-partner's partner before he died, and his dislike of me had been instant and intense and, to me at least, inexplicable. Since then it had only expanded and intensified. He was convinced I was crooked—something I had believed of him a time or two, before eventually deciding I was giving him too much credit.

"Folsom's not here," he said, "so you don't get no free pass to my crime scene."

Evidently, he was unaware of my falling out with Folsom. Was everyone?

I knew it was pointless to argue with him, but I couldn't help myself.

"If it's who I think it is, I may have some information that'll help you," I said.

"You could have the murderer handcuffed in your car and I wouldn't want a thing from you. Not a goddamn thing."

"Well, at least you're reasonable. Good to see you still put the work first."

The elevator doors opened and David Howell gingerly stepped out.

"Hiya Jimmy," he said. "Butch."

"Morning," I said.

"So you two have met," Butch said. "Be careful, Dave. You're new. I'd hate for you to get off on the wrong foot—" As if he only realized right then what he had said, he looked down at David's bad leg then quickly away, then said, "So to speak."

He shook his head. "We ready to have a look?"

"He was just leaving," Butch said, "but you and me, yeah."

"Why're you leaving so soon?" David asked.

"Because Butch wishes it so."

"What?" he said, then looked over at Butch. "Why?"

"He's . . . he's private. Don't need to be here."

"Folsom wants him to help out with it. Told me to make sure he gets our full cooperation."

"Tell you what then," Butch said, starting to walk toward the elevator, "you two help yourselves to anything you like. I've seen all I need to. Been better if the silly old man would've died from that gunshot than to hang around and ruin the department."

"I'll be sure to let him know you think so," David said.

"You do that," he said, as he punched the elevator button. "You're as bad as he is."

David and I walked down the hotel corridor to the room with the open door where the two cops were standing.

"Whatta we got?" David asked.

We glanced inside.

"Male victim. Single shotgun blast to the head. Does not appear to be self-inflicted."

Inside the room there was blood on the bed and the wall, but there was no body. A young cop was tagging and bagging what remained.

"Where the hell is the body?" David asked.

"Already taken away. We're just waiting for the rest of the evidence and belongings to be bagged and we're out of here."

David shook his head. "Butch," he said in disgust.

We stepped inside, careful to keep back from the bed and avoid the blood.

"Tell me," David said.

He shrugged. "Just here to gather up everything. Got nothing to do with the investigation."

"Obviously, we don't either," David said.

We looked around for a few minutes.

An open suitcase in the corner had only a few random clothes in it. Everything else had been picked up and placed in bags. The bags were stacked against the wall over near the door.

As we were leaving, David asked the uniform at the door, "Got an ID?"

"Bennett," he said. "The boxer."

Riding the elevator back down with Howell, I wondered again about him. What was he playing at? Why antagonize Butch? Had something already happened between the two of them? Could he just tell Butch was a blunt bully? Or was it something else? And why lie? Why tell him Folsom said to give me full access to the case? Was he ingratiating himself to me for other reasons? I couldn't yet guess at what ulterior motives he could have—unless he were acting as a surrogate for Henry Folsom somehow.

"Seemed sort of fast for the body to be moved," I said.

He nodded.

"Wonder why it was and who was behind it?"

"Plan to find out," he said.

The doors opened and we stepped out.

Spotting Francis Stevens over in the far corner of the lobby, I walked over to talk to him. Howell followed.

"Thanks for callin' me," I said.

He looked from me to Howell.

"He's okay," I said. "Speak freely."

"I tried you for a while before I got you. Most of the

action was done by the time you showed up."

"I noticed. How long since they brought the body down?"

He glanced across the way to the clock hanging on the wall. "Half hour."

"Did you go in the room when the body was first found?"

He hesitated a moment, acting as if something near the front door caught his attention. When I followed his gaze, I saw there was nothing there.

"Well, did ya?"

"Never seen a dead body before," he said. "Just wanted to . . . you know . . . sneak a peek."

"And?"

"I feel bad for the fella, I do. But it was a sight to see. Glad I did. All that blood . . . and his head . . . and neck and . . . They got him but good. *Pow.* Right in the kisser."

"So his face was gone?"

"No, sir. Most of his neck was though. Some of his chin, but no, you could see his face pretty good."

I looked at Howell.

He looked back and I could tell we were thinking the same thing—and had been. Thinking that it had been a shot to the face to hide the identity. Now that we knew that wasn't the case, our minds were going in different directions.

"So you could see his face clearly?" I asked.

"Not really. Lotta blood on it. Part of it hidden by the pillow."

"But you could tell it was Jeff Bennett?"

"*I* couldn't," he said.

"Who said that's who it was?"

"I heard a lotta people say it. Maid. Manager. Cops."

Though he had yet to say a word, I could tell David Howell was focused on the conversation. His quiet concentration was palpable.

"You couldn't because you couldn't see enough of his face, or because it didn't look like him?" I asked.

He shrugged. "Just looked different to me. Maybe it was being dead or the blast from the gun . . . but I didn't think it was him."

"Okay," I said. "Thanks Francis."

"But it *was* him. Everything in the room was his—hell, his name was on most of it. And everyone else said it was him. I just . . ."

"Whose room was it?"

"Was supposed to be empty."

"So why'd the maid go in?" Howell asked.

He shrugged. "They check 'em and freshin' 'em up every few days when they're not bein' used. Maybe that, but I don't know for sure."

"She still here?" Howell asked.

"Sent her home."

I withdrew a five and slipped it to him. "Nicely done," I said. "Keep it up."

"Whatta you think?" Howell asked.

We were still standing in the back corner of the lobby. Frances had just hurried off to help an arriving couple with their luggage.

I shrugged. "Not sure what to make of it. Might not have been able to tell even if we had gotten to see the body, but I would've liked the chance."

He nodded. "The whole thing is . . ."

I waited for him to say something else, to finish the thought, but he never did.

"Plenty that's off," I said. "Question is whether it just seems that way because of how little we know or if the more we find out the more off it will become."

"Was thinkin' there for a minute that he had been shot in the face to cover up who it really was," he said, "but guess that's not the case after all."

"Won't know for sure until we see the body. Think you can arrange that?"

He nodded. "Shouldn't be a problem."

"Anything Butch is within a mile of is a problem."

Before he could respond, a middle-aged man carrying a briefcase stepped over.

He was wide and thick without being fat exactly.

"Mr. Riley?" he said.

I nodded.

"I'm Pierce Ames," he said. "I'm—or rather was—Harry Lewis's attorney. Well, I guess I still am. I just meant . . . I now work for the estate. It's absolutely urgent that I speak to Mrs. Lewis. I'm told you might be able to help with that."

"I might," I said.

"I'm gonna go see if I can find out what's going on," Howell said, "and see if I can get us a look at that body. I'll let you two talk."

He walked away.

"What's this about?" I asked.

"I understand the Lewises weren't on the best of terms when Mr. Lewis died, but . . . if he ever had any intention of doing something about it—"

"Oh, he had plenty of intention."

"Well he didn't get around to it."

"He got around to plenty, pal. Trust me on that."

"She stands to . . . ah . . . inherit a great deal. Harry—ah, Mr. Lewis—never made a new will. She gets it all. And all is a lot."

I was suddenly and inexplicably angry with this attorney.

He was giving me some genuinely good news, but that was not how I was hearing it. All I could think about was all the trouble Harry had caused us, all the trouble his money would if given the chance.

He withdrew his card from his coat pocket and handed it to me.

"Can you help?"

"I might be able to," I said.

"I want to reiterate: It's good news. It's an inheritance. A huge one. That's it. Nothing more. Nothing else."

The front door flung open and Kay Hudson rushed in, her eyes frantically scanning the lobby.

"Excuse me," I said to Ames. "I'll be in touch."

When Kay's wild eyes landed on me, she ran over to me.

"Is it true?"

"Breathe," I said, touching her shoulder with my hand. "Take a breath, try to calm down, and listen very carefully to what I'm saying."

She took in a deep breath, let it out in a long, loud sigh, and attempted to settle down.

"We don't know who it is," I said. "There is a body, but I haven't seen it yet, and there's conflicting information about the identity."

"But it could be him?"

"It's possible," I said, "but it's just as possible it's not. I know it's difficult, but if you can just wait until we know before you—"

"I knew this was going to happen," she said. "I knew it. Where's the body? I can help with the ID."

"It's not here," I said. "Already been removed."

"Well, take me to where it is. I can—"

"Miss Hudson, I have to tell you," I said, "your reaction doesn't strike me as that of a concerned colleague."

"What?"

"Have you been having an affair with Jeff? Are you two . . ."

"No," she said. "I swear it. We've never even touched beyond a handshake. Any concern is for both Jeff and his wife. Any idea where she is? *How* she is?"

"Not yet, no," I said, "but I'm working on it."

She had visibly calmed down now, her strength and self-possession having returned.

David Howell walked back over and I introduced them.

"Miss Hudson is a colleague of Jeff and Rebecca's and has offered to identify the body if we need her to."

"That would be helpful," he said. "It'll be a while before we can do it, but I'll set it up."

While waiting to meet David Howell and Kay Hudson at the morgue, Lauren and I paid a visit to the law office of Pierce Ames.

His office was located in the back of Harry's bank. Thankfully, there was a side door that led straight in so we didn't have to walk past Harry's old office or be exposed out in the open for more than a moment.

After pulling up and parking on the curb right in front of the door, I jumped out, checked the area, then got Lauren out and rushed her across the few steps of the sidewalk and through the door.

"Thank you so much for coming," Ames said. "So good of you to bring her."

He had met us in the small outer office occupied by his secretary.

"If you'd like to have a seat out here," he said to me, "this shouldn't take long. Brenda here will be happy to get you some coffee or—"

"Jimmy's coming in with us," Lauren said.

Her voice was strong and firm, but there wasn't anything emotional in it. She was just stating a fact, not arguing a point or responding to a slight.

"Are you sure?" Ames said. "This is—"

"We really don't have long," Lauren said. "We need to get on with this."

"Of course," he said. "As you wish."

There was something about Ames, a sort of prissiness and formality and inauthenticity that I found annoying. Of course, in fairness, I found this entire ordeal annoying and angry-making, so that may have contributed to my dislike of the man.

When we were seated in his office—him behind his too-large desk, us in the two chairs in front of it—he looked at the file folder on his desk, then at Lauren.

I wondered if he had anything to do with Harry's depravity and criminality or his plot to denigrate and destroy Lauren.

"What all did you do for Harry Lewis?" I asked.

"This is it," he said. "Just his will. He had a variety of attorneys for a variety of interests. I specialize in wills and last testaments, that sort of thing."

It occurred to me that as difficult as I was finding this, Lauren may have been even more so.

"You okay?" I asked.

She was seated to the right of me, so I had to reach across my body with my left to touch her on the back, an awkward movement for a simple gesture of support.

She nodded, her eyes narrowing slightly as they found mine.

"Well then," Ames said. "Let's get to it, shall we?"

He looked at the open folder on his desk again, then closed it—and something about it looked rehearsed.

"The simple fact is you get everything, Mrs. Lewis,"

he said. "Not to put too fine a point on it. All his property, including your lovely home on the bay, all his stocks and bonds, his life insurance, his CDs, all the cash in his accounts. Everything. It's an old will, and though he had expressed a desire to make another, he never actually did."

"I thought he had," Lauren said. "I thought . . ."

"The estate is worth in excess of three and a half million dollars," he said. "You are a very wealthy woman. The wealthiest in town, in fact. My guess is that Lady Bird Bennett is second, but I bet she barely has over a million."

With this last statement some of his affect fell away and more of the real Pierce Ames became visible.

"Congratulations, Mrs. Lewis," he said. "I have quite a few documents I need you to sign but I'm afraid all of them are not ready yet. But you're welcome back in the house—I assume you're not staying there because I've tried calling on you there several times—and I can get you a line of credit at the bank in any amount you like."

"Can we have a moment?" Lauren said. "Would you mind excusing us for—"

"Of course," he said, tripping over himself to get up and get out of his own office because the newly wealthy lady wished it so.

When he had closed the door behind him, she turned to me.

"Wow," she said, exhaling a long sigh. "I just can't . . . This is so unexpected."

I didn't say anything, just listened, just let her process what had just happened.

"I guess all our financial worries are over," she said.

"Don't kid yourself," I said.

"I just meant . . ."

"I know," I said, "but this is the beginning not the end of worries and troubles. They may be different than the ones you have now, but there will be far more of them and they will be far more intense."

"You?" she said.

"Huh?"

"You said *you* not *we*."

"It's *your* money."

"We're a *we*," she said. "It's not *my* money. It's *ours*. I'm yours. You're mine. We're . . ."

"None of this is easy for me," I said. "I'm sorry if I'm not saying or doing the right things."

"You're not saying or doing anything wrong," she said. "This isn't easy for me either."

I nodded.

I realized I was feeling much more than I was expressing to her, that I apologized for not saying or doing the right things because of what I was feeling.

"What is it?" she said. "Tell me."

"Can we talk about it later?" I asked. "I really need to get to the morgue for the identification."

"Okay," she said, "but could you at least tell me a little? Give me something."

"I could never live in Harry's house."

"I wouldn't ask you to," she said. "I couldn't live there either."

I nodded.

"What else?"

"It can wait."

"Tell me," she said.

"I want nothing to do with Harry's money. Nothing."

"It's not Harry's money anymore. It's ours. Think of all the good we can do with it. Think of the—"

"I can't right now," I said. "I really need to go."

Chapter 25

"Are you sure you're okay to do this?" I asked.

I was standing in a small, sterile hallway inside the morgue with Kay Hudson.

She nodded.

I wanted to watch her reaction to viewing the body, but I also felt for her and didn't want to be inhumane—even regarding a task she insisted on undertaking.

David Howell had gone to get someone to help us with the viewing.

"I have to know," she said. "Have to see for myself. I just can't believe he's dead. And if he is, where is Becky? What has happened to her? We've got to find her, got to—"

"We will."

When Howell rejoined us he looked even more somber than before.

"I'm sorry," he said to Kay, "but I'm afraid it is him. No need to identify the body. His mother did it about half an hour ago."

"So it's him," she said. "He's . . . really . . ."

She seemed genuinely upset but not overly so—not nearly as undone as she was earlier at the Dixie.

"I'm sorry," I said.

"We've got to find Becky," she said. "Poor thing. She . . ."

"His wife is missing too?" Howell asked.

I nodded. "Seems so."

"I still want to see him," Kay said. "Still have to. Won't really believe he's dead until I do, and since I'm already here anyway . . ."

Howell looked at me.

I gave him a small shrug and a nod.

"Okay," he said. "I'll go set it up."

"That's not him," she said.

The mortician had just pulled back the sheet, folding it down to reveal the face of the body on the table.

The room was bright, white, and cold.

The mortician was a weary-looking middle-aged man, tall and egg-headed, his pallor running to gray.

"What?" Howell said.

"That's not him. That's not Jeff Bennett. Only looks like him a little. Did you pull out the wrong body?"

"Ma'am," the mortician said, "I assure you this is the right body."

"And I assure you, this is *not* Jeff Bennett."

"Perhaps in death his appearance has altered to the point of—"

"This is not Jeff Bennett."

"His mother says it is."

Kay looked over at me. "Well, then she's lying. I don't know why she is, but she is."

I nodded. "We'll find out."

"What possible reason would Lady Bird Bennett

have for lying about her son?" the mortician asked.

"You're absolutely sure?" Howell asked her.

"His calf," she said. "His right calf. He's got a long cut that runs the length of it from a rusty wire fence in Burma. He tried to jump it while we were there covering the war recently and a barb ripped open his skin nearly all the way down his calf."

"Can we see his calf?" Howell asked.

"What will it prove?" the mortician said. "Whether it's there or not . . ."

He moved around to the right side of the table and expertly folded back the sheet to reveal only the right leg—and not even all of it. He then turned the pale leg just enough to reveal most of the calf.

There was no cut.

"See?" she said. "She's lying. That's not Jeff's leg. This is not Jeff Bennett. Something is very much amiss."

"Whatta you think?" David Howell asked.

We were in the hallway, near the same spot where Kay and I had stood before. She was in the restroom. We were waiting for her.

"Someone's lying," I said.

He looked at me quizzically, as if he couldn't quite tell whether I was being serious or not.

I was tempted to smile, but I didn't.

"Insightful," he said.

Points for Dave. I wasn't sure he had it in him.

"It's a gift."

"Any insight into which one is lying and why?"

I shook my head. "Even my gifts have their

limitations."

"Guess it's not possible one of 'em is just mistaken," he said.

"Hard to see how," I said.

"If it's really not Jeff Bennett," he said, "then not only do we still have to find him but we need to figure out who this guy is and who killed him too."

"What're you, a cop or something?"

Kay Hudson returned and we began walking out of the building, Howell and I both careful to check the area outside before we did—though she didn't seem to notice.

"How much does the body in there resemble Jeff?" I asked.

She shrugged. "Some."

"Enough for a distraught mother to misidentify her son?" I asked.

She shook her head. "Absolutely not."

Chapter 26

When we left the morgue, Kay and I drove over to the Cove to Lady Bird Bennett's while Howell went back to the station to check in with Folsom.

To no one's surprise, Mrs. Bennett refused to see us.

"Tell her we only need a moment," Kay said.

We were standing outside the enormous front door, which had just been opened slightly a second time for the maid to tell us that the lady of the house would be unable to see us just then.

"Ma'am," the maid said, "she's just lost her son. She is unable to—"

"But—"

"We'll come back another time," I said.

"Please make an appointment first, sir."

"Why you little—" Kay began.

"We certainly will," I said. "Thank—"

She closed the large door with a loud reverberating thud before I could finish.

"See?" Kay said. "She won't see us because she knows I know that's not Jeff."

"Or she thinks her only son is dead and she's too

upset."

Walking back to the car, I noticed the chauffeur over near the garage working on one of Lady Bird's vehicles—a different one from the '42 black Nash Ambassador I had seen before.

"Go ahead and get in the car," I said to Kay. "I'll be right back."

She started to say something but I didn't give her the chance. Having given her a little push toward the car, I was heading back up the drive toward the garage.

The chauffeur, a short, smallish fortyish-looking man with a dark complexion and short wavy hair, was still wearing the white uniform I had seen him in before.

The hood of the Packard was up and he was standing on an apple crate and leaning in over the left quarter panel making some sort of adjustment with a wrench.

It was odd to see a grown man having to stand on a box to reach the engine of a car and it occurred to me that he looked more like a jockey than a chauffeur.

"Afternoon," I said as I walked up.

He nodded but didn't say anything.

"Car trouble?" I asked.

"'Man born of woman is of few days and full of trouble,'" he said.

It was obvious that it was something he said often.

"So not just car trouble, but . . ."

"Life is trouble," he said, then glancing over his shoulder back at the house added, "even for the rich."

"Yeah," I said, "I'm a very wealthy man and it hasn't insulated me from . . . the slings and arrows of outrageous fortune."

His eyes darted to what remained of my right arm.

I followed his glance. "I chose to take arms against the sea."

"The sea?"

"Of troubles."

He nodded, but I could tell he didn't get it, and he went back to work with the wrench.

I had thought, based on his quote from the book of Job, he might appreciate a little Shakespeare. I was wrong.

"I'm Jimmy," I said.

He nodded and grunted something that wasn't his name.

"You are?"

He paused, looked at me, started to extend his hand, but instead held it up to show the grease and grime.

"Lawrence Vickery," he said.

"I know you're busy, Lawrence," I said, "so I'll only trouble you for a minute."

He gave no indication he appreciated my use of *trouble* again, but undeterred I slogged on.

"Mrs. Bennett has hired me to find out where Rebecca Bennett is," I said. "Where's the last place you drove her?"

"Mrs. Bennett?"

"The younger."

"Huh?"

"Rebecca. Where's the last place you drove Rebecca Bennett?"

He shook his head, glanced nervously over his shoulder toward the house, then said, "I didn't . . . I mean to say I haven't driven Miss Rebecca anywhere recently."

"Really?"

He nodded. "Why?"

"What about Jeff?"

"Same," he said. "Only Mrs. Bennett lately."

"You sure?"

"Yes, sir. Now, if you don't mind, I need to get this finished."

I started to walk away, then turned back. "What'd you do before you became Lady Bird Bennett's chauffeur?"

He didn't respond, just remained intensely focused on his work.

"Did it involve horses?"

He jerked around toward me, jumped off the crate, and came at me, the gleaming and grimy wrench held out in front of him.

"It wasn't a crack," I said. "I really wondered."

"You need to leave," he said. "Now. And you need to learn to keep your mouth shut. Better not say anything like that to anyone. And you say it in front of Mrs. Bennett, I'll kill you."

"That's cute but don't let the missing arm fool you," I said. "I don't kill so easy."

Chapter 27

Was it any wonder I loved Lauren the way I did?

On the same day she learned that she had inherited three and a half million dollars to become the richest woman in town, she spent her evening volunteering at the USO Club, helping those in need, giving to her country, serving soldiers, being true to who she is regardless of her station or financial statement.

I had arrived early to look around the parking lot, to ensure it was safe before she came out.

I was tired and frustrated and getting nowhere on either case. All I wanted to do was get in a warm bed with Lauren somewhere safe. And stay there.

When she walked through the doors, weary but attempting like hell not to show it, I was waiting for her. She threaded her arm around mine and we slowly made our way to the car, which was illegally parked nearby.

"Are you okay?" I asked.

She nodded.

"You overdid it, didn't you?"

She smiled. "Maybe a little."

"Let's get you . . ."

I had started to say *home* but realized we didn't have one.

". . . into a warm bath and then bed," I said.

I helped her into the car, then ran around, got behind the wheel, and pulled away.

As much as I appreciated her desire to do for others, it occurred to me that her work at the USO not only took her away from me more now, but might speed up or even bring about her eventual and ultimate departure, and it made me angry.

"Given how you're feeling right now, don't you think you're trying to do too much?"

"I won't overdo it. I promise. But I have to do something."

"I think you already are," I said.

"If I overdid it tonight, I won't make that mistake again."

In a very real way she was risking her life to do what she was doing. She hadn't recovered from her life-threatening illness yet. In fact, she might not ever fully recover. And yet, she insisted on pushing herself to volunteer.

She was doing all this at such risk, and I was doing next to nothing for the war effort. It had to bother her, had to cause her to think I was . . . I couldn't imagine what she must think of me.

"Is it worth your health?" I asked.

"No, of course not. You're sweet, but I really am fine."

"You're risking so much to do this," I said.

"I was thinking about the money while I was there tonight," she said.

I could feel myself knotting up.

"I was thinking I want to do so much more than I am, more than I am able to, and I thought of . . . Do you have any idea how much good we could do with it?"

"I know that's what everybody always says at the beginning," I said.

"You really don't think we could handle it?" she said. "Don't forget, I've had money before. I did okay. I had loads of it when we met—when you fell in love with me."

"It's blood money, Lauren."

"How do you know?"

"I knew its most recent owner," I said. "But even if I didn't, most money is—and nearly all fortunes. And if it wasn't before, it is now. I killed Harry. I'm not gonna profit from that. I'm not gonna—"

"I'd say you already have."

"Sure, but only because it saved your life and us the hassle of dealing with a divorce."

She shook her head, frowned, then fell silent.

We were quiet a while.

"I disagree with you," she said.

"I know."

"It's not a position I'm accustomed to."

I nodded.

"What are we going to do?"

"Figure it out," I said.

"And if we can't?"

"We can."

"God, I love you," she said.

"I love you."

"But I'm worried. This worries me. I'm not sure I can say why exactly."

I didn't say anything.

"What if we took half?"

I shook my head.

"A quarter then?"

I gave her the same response.

"How much then?"

"None."

"What if *I* just take some? Just a fraction . . . and that way you never have to—"

"What happened to you and I being a *we*?"

"*We* are. That's what this is all about."

"Then you can't take any without it being *we* who takes it. So no."

"You're being unreasonable," she said. "I can't talk about this anymore right now."

Chapter 28

"Where you?" Clip asked.

I was standing beside him the next morning in the Bay High School gym watching Freddy train, so I knew his question wasn't literal.

"Huh?"

"Where were you just then?" he asked.

I shrugged. "Got a lot goin' on."

"Seen you with a lot more not half as distracted. It ain't Freddy or Jeff or no Japs got you like this. Only one thing make you this way."

I smiled, grateful to have a friend who knew me so well.

"Thought Lauren was doin' better," he said. "Somethin' change?"

I shook my head.

"Dis 'bout her helpin' over to the USO club?"

I shook my head again.

"Then what?"

I told him.

"You da only motherfucker in the world be sad 'bout bein' rich."

"I'm not rich."

"She rich, you rich."

I shook my head. "Ain't takin' any of Harry's money."

"You already have. You forget how we funded finding Lauren?"

"That was different."

"Hell, yeah, it was. Now it her money."

"I just got her back," I said.

"And?"

"Nothin' can fuck up a relationship faster than money."

"I can think of a few things," he said.

I didn't respond.

With no one around but us and Gus, Freddy was going at it hard and looked like an actual contender.

"What is it you think money gonna change?"

"Everything?"

"Didn't she have all this the first time y'all got together?"

"Harry did."

"And she was married to Harry."

"Yeah."

"So she had it—or had access to it."

I shrugged.

"You think she won't need you as much? Have more options . . . so what, she'll leave you? You think she only been with you 'cause she was broke?"

"No."

He didn't say anything and we fell quiet again for a moment.

"Want nothin' to do with that world," I said.

"Even if it Lauren's?"

"If she wants that," I said, "she doesn't want me."

He nodded. "I see. So you wantin' your world mean you don't want her?"

He was right. It didn't mean that. Not at all.

Before I could say anything, Saul entered the gym and walked over to us.

He had a folded piece of paper in his right hand. He held it up when he reached us.

"Got another one today," he said.

Clip nodded toward me. "That his department. I just help people with they love life. And occasionally shoot somebody."

He handed me the paper. I carefully unfolded and examined it.

Using words cut from various newspapers and magazines, it looked more like a ransom note than anything else. "Take your nigger out of the fight or he is not the only one who will die."

All the words except for *nigger* were single cuttings from a variety of newspapers and magazines. But *nigger* was formed from splicing together letters from three different publications, giving it an eerie exaggerated look the others, bizarre as they were, didn't have.

"First time he's threatened me too," Saul said.

"That change anything for you?" Clip asked.

Saul shrugged.

"Where was it?"

"Slipped beneath my hotel room door when I woke up this morning," he said. "He knows where I live. Could've killed me in my sleep last night."

"Where have the others been?"

"Here. Mostly."

I looked at the note again.

"Based on the other notes, I'd say it's the same person, that he's fairly educated, and either well read or has access to a lot of different papers and magazines."

"You thinkin' 'bout backin' out now?" Clip asked Saul.

"Maybe. I don't know. It's just . . ."

"It okay for Freddy to be in the bulls-eye but not you?"

"I'm not sayin' that. It's not like that. I just—*we*—just have to weigh everything. Figure out the best plan. Or . . ."

"Or?" Clip asked, an edge of challenge in his voice.

"You could catch him before he hurts anyone."

"We're working on it," I said. "We'll set up at your hotel and here at night and see if we can't grab him when he makes his next delivery."

Saul nodded.

"It important that Freddy fight," Clip said. "That he back up what he said in the paper. It matters."

"It does," Saul said.

"If it do for him it do for you."

"I'm not saying it doesn't," Saul said. "Just that we have to figure out exactly how much it matters. Is it worth our lives?"

"If it ain't, why y'all doin' it then?"

"Good question. That's the kind of question this kind of situation raises."

"Is there any pattern to when he leaves them?" I asked.

Saul seemed to think about it.

"Always at night. I find them waiting for me the next

morning."

"Certain days?"

He appeared to think about it some more.

"Different days of the week," he said.

Suddenly, seemingly out of nowhere, something occurred to me.

"Was Freddy in the paper yesterday?"

Saul nodded. "Small piece."

"Does the guy leave them on nights when Freddy's been in that day's paper?"

His eyes grew wide and his face lit up. "He must. I've had the thought when I've read them I need to get Freddy to tone it down some. We'd have to check it to make sure, but . . ."

"What if he's using Freddy's words against him?" I said.

Clip nodded. "Could be, but he ain't tellin' him to shut the fuck up. He tellin' him not to fight."

"You're right," I said. "Still, if he's doin' it when Freddy's in the paper, it'd narrow down when we have to lose sleep setting up on Saul."

"Hell, if it's true, we can pick the day," Clip said. "Fast Mouth Freddy never at a loss for words."

Chapter 29

"Whatta you think Jimmy?" Folsom asked.

We were in his office discussing the discrepancies between the two different identifications of the body.

David Howell and Butch were already seated across from Folsom's desk when I arrived. I was standing over near the small bookshelf on the right wall.

I shrugged.

"Somebody mistaken? Or is somebody lying?" he asked.

"Don't see how it could be a mistake," I said. "Kay Hudson says it couldn't be."

"She says the wealthiest woman in town is lying," he said.

"Second."

"Huh?"

"Second wealthiest woman," I said.

"Really? Who's the first?"

"Doesn't matter."

"What?"

"Nothing. Yeah, she says she's lying."

"She say why?" he asked.

"Not really, no. Just that she's crooked and up to something."

"With all due respect," Butch said, "we need to be talking to them. Not relying on a . . . on an amateur to do it for us."

This was Butch on his best behavior. He would only go so far with Folsom around.

"All due respect, huh?" Folsom said. "How much is that, do you figure?"

"Plenty enough for you, sir," he said. "More than enough."

"Jimmy is not an amateur," Folsom said. "He was one of us. Still would be if he hadn't gotten his arm blown off in the line of duty. He's a hell of an investigator, and I trust him more than anyone I know, so—"

"Fine," Butch said, "but what about a conflict of interest because one of 'em's his client?"

"Which one?" Folsom asked me.

"Actually, technically, both."

"*Jesus*," Butch said.

"Language, Detective," Folsom said.

"Sorry, but . . . come on. He's working for *both* of 'em and we're supposed to . . . I was wrong. He doesn't have a conflict of interest. He's got several of them."

"Who do you believe?" Folsom asked.

"I'm inclined to believe Kay Hudson," I said, "but I haven't talked to Mrs. Bennett yet. Not since she identified the body as her son. She wouldn't see me last night. I'm going to try again this afternoon."

"Why would she lie?" David said. "She'd have to know it'd get out."

"The rich are different," Butch said. "Probably

figured she could buy off someone if it came to that later."

"For once I agree with Butch," I said.

"Then I take it back."

"We have to be very careful on this," Folsom said. "I'm not saying don't investigate, not saying don't follow the evidence wherever it leads. But *I am* saying be sure. We can't even hint at an accusation against someone like Lady Bird Bennett without being absolutely sure."

Butch started to say something, but Folsom continued.

"And it's not special treatment because she's rich," Folsom said. "It's prudence. Wisdom. We want to find whoever killed him—whoever *he* is—and someone like her can make it very difficult for us. She can't stop us—I won't let her—but she can make this far harder than it has to be."

He paused for a moment and Butch started to say something again.

"How can I put this?" Folsom said. "This whole thing—particularly dealing with someone like Lady Bird Bennett . . . requires more delicacy than you're capable of, Butch. I'll assign you to a different case. David, you take the lead, but from here on out I'll talk to her. I'll take care of interviewing her. And I want everything related to the case run by me before it happens. Not afterward. Understand?"

David nodded. "Yes sir."

Butch didn't say anything.

"Detective?"

"Yeah, I got it," Butch said. "I don't mind none. A case is a case is a case. I'd rather not deal with the likes of her anyhows."

"Jimmy, I'd like you to try to talk to her again. Let's see how that goes. Depending on that . . . will determine my approach. In the meantime I'd like to talk to Kay Hudson. Can you bring her in?"

"Sure."

"And David, find me an alternative way to get a positive ID on the body. Dental records. Medical records. Something."

"Yes, sir. Already working on it. Should have something soon."

"Mrs. Bennett ain't home," Lawrence Vickery said when I stepped out of my car.

He was walking toward me from the garage.

"Don't call her that," I said.

"Huh?"

"Her late husband's mother will always be Mrs. Bennett."

A smile ticked the corner of his lips but he resisted it, tightening his mouth, pursing his lips, suppressing even the slightest sign of amusement.

"So where is Birdie?" I said.

"Away."

"And how'd she get there since her car and driver are here?"

"The lady's transportation arrangements are none of your concern."

I turned and started toward the front door. "I'll just check for myself. Not doubting you. Not at all. Just being thorough. Birdie expects no less from all her employees. I know you know all about that."

"Do what you like, mister," he said. "No one will

come to the door."

He was right. No one did.

"Told you," he said when I returned.

"Where is Jeff Bennett?" I said.

"Still at the morgue, I think."

"Where is his wife?"

"I'm not sure."

"His mother?"

"Somewhere safe and quiet, dealing with her grief."

"I know you think you're protecting her, but you're not," I said. "Next visit will be from the cops."

"I'm pretty sure Birdie owns them," he said. "Now if that's all . . . I have work to do."

Before I could tell him that wasn't all, a black car pulled into the driveway and Miles Lydecker's elephantine twins got out and walked toward us.

"I'm kinda busy right now, fellas," I said.

"Not here for you, Riley," the one closest to me said.

"So beat it," the other one added.

"You need to come with us, Larry."

No wonder Vickery had reacted to my remark about horses. He must have thought I was making a crack about his gambling problem.

"Now's not a good time, fellas," Vickery said.

The one near him drew a gun, pointed it at him, and said, "How about now? Is now better?"

The one closer to me turned and aimed his withdrawn weapon at me. I lifted my arm.

"Thought I told you to beat it," the other one said.

"What I was just about to do," I said, beginning to back down the driveway toward my car, my arm still raised.

"Wait," Vickery said.

"For what?"

He tried to think of something. Finally he said, "Help me."

"With what?"

I continued easing down the driveway until I reached my car, got in, cranked it, and pulled away as the two behemoths were loading Vickery into their car.

Turning the wrong way on Bunker's Cove, I drove up about a quarter mile or so and turned around. By the time I reached Lady Bird Bennett's driveway again, they were several car lengths in front of me headed toward town.

I followed.

I had to slow down several times not to get too close to them and speed up several others not to lose them.

They turned left on Cherry Street, past the Cove Hotel, curved right onto Beach Drive, crossed over Massalina Bayou, then took a left on Harrison.

Traffic on all the streets was steady, but only Harrison was crowded, its sidewalks as congested with pedestrians as its street with cars.

The day was nice and bright, cold but not too.

They drove to a quiet corner at the end of Harrison near the water, where Miles Lydecker was waiting for them in sunglasses, a buttoned-up overcoat, and a gray hat he had to keep a hand on to keep it from blowing into the bay.

I parked across the way, and by the time I reached them, all four men were standing in a small circle on the sidewalk between the hood of Lydecker's car and the guardrail.

"How much he into you for?" I said to Miles as I walked up.

"Enough to warrant a little chat when he misses a payment. Whatta you want, Riley?"

"I was having a little chat with him myself when these little bastards showed up and interrupted."

"Popular guy," Miles said.

I nodded.

"What's he involved in?" Lydecker asked. "Anything I'd be interested in?"

I shook my head.

"Anything that'd keep him from paying what he owes?"

I shrugged. "How much does he owe?"

"Let's say I have a substantial investment in him and I don't want anything hindering my return." He turned suddenly to Vickery. "Do you have my money?"

"Not on me, no sir," he said, "but I can get it."

"'You can get it' as in if I have my associates run you to where it is, you can secure it and return here and promptly pay me, or as in 'Mr. Lydecker, sir, I'm good for it. Just give a little more time. I can get it. I can. I just need more time. Please, sir. Please don't kill me.'"

"The second one. Mostly. But it's true. I can get it. You know who I work for. You know I'm good for it."

"You've never been this late before, never owed so much before. I don't want to be mistaken about you but fear I may have misjudged and let this go too far."

"You haven't. I swear it."

"Okay," Lydecker said. "I guess we shall see. Break the little finger on his left hand."

Quicker than I thought they were capable, the two men were on Vickery—one holding, the other breaking—snapping his little finger like popping the head off a shrimp. A small crunch of bone and yelp of pain followed by profanity pouring from the little man's mouth.

"I'm more than reasonable," Lydecker said. "I gave you only a small reminder. Nothing to interfere with your ability to work and get me my money. I trust you can find your way back home."

"I'll take him," I said. "Give us a chance to finish our conversation."

"I'd rather walk," Vickery said.

"So, Miles," I said. "What happens if Lawrence doesn't pay?"

"You mean at all?"

"Yes."

"He is taken off the ledger. For good."

I turned to Vickery. "And what do you think happens if I tell Lady Bird Bennett about your little gambling problem?"

"It's not little," Lydecker said.

"You son of a—"

"Wait for me in the car," I said.

"You heard the man," Lydecker said.

"Can I have a minute?" I asked.

"Sure. You two wait in the car too."

"You said you wanted Freddy fighting," I said. "So who wouldn't?"

"Pardon?"

"If it's in your interest for him to fight, whose interest is it in for him not to fight? I mean from your world."

"My world?"

"I don't mean other fighters or promoters. Anybody in your racket who wouldn't want him to fight."

He shrugged. "Nobody I can think of. Men in my, ah, line of work typically only try to influence outcome. Who's involved is only relevant in the way it affects the spread."

I nodded and thought about it.

"Hard to imagine it doesn't have something to do with Gentleman Jeff bowing out."

"True."

"Sorry," he said. "Can't help you with anything but the obvious."

"If Freddy does fight and doesn't throw it, will he be permanently taken off the ledger too?"

"Whatta you think? Ol' little Larry over there owes peanuts compared to Fuckup Freddy."

"Where is Birdie?" I asked.

"Inside her house, but she won't open the door for you."

Lawrence Vickery and I were on Beach Drive in my car, heading back toward Bunker's Cove and his place of employment. He was in obvious pain from the broken finger, but to his credit he was doing his best not to let on.

"Where is Jeff?" I asked.

"You really don't think that's him in the morgue?"

"You tell me."

"I don't know. I haven't heard anything. Mrs. Bennett's sure acting like it is."

"By hiding in her house?" I said. "Wouldn't she do that same thing if she were trying to avoid people like me and the police?"

"She can handle people just fine—especially people

like you and the police."

"Birdie said Jeff was convalescing at a facility before she said he was dead. Any truth in it?"

He nodded.

"Where's the place?"

"West. Middle of nowhere. Near Fort Walton. Went in the middle of the night. Not sure I could find it again. No need if he's dead, right?"

I shrugged.

"Hey pal, I'm tellin' you everything I know. You're not gonna foul me up with the bitch, are you? I really need this job. My life fuckin' depends on it."

"Where is Rebecca?"

"I drove her and Jeff and Mrs. B over there that night. Only Mrs. B came home with me."

"She's in the same place?"

"Was. At least that's the last time I saw her."

"What do you know about Kay Hudson?"

"Nothin'. Heard her name a few times. Not much else."

"If the victim is not Jeff, any idea who it is?"

He shook his head. "But I'll tell you what I do know. I know that something is very wrong with Jeff Bennett. He's always been off. Long as I've known him. But now . . . he's . . . I don't know. It's like the war did something to him. If he's not the one who's dead, wouldn't surprise me in the least if he's the one who checked whoever it is out of the Dixie Sherman and into the big hotel in the sky."

Chapter 31

While waiting for Lauren to come out of the USO club, I reread the notes and papers left by Jeff Bennett in the Dixie.

Though most of the notes where incoherent and made little to no sense at all, I was able to make out several of the names and the connections between them.

Buried within the many names I didn't recognize were several that I did. Among them the mayor, a couple of county commissioners, a couple of cops, a few wealthy individuals—and a few sycophants aspiring to be them.

Like Lee Perkins's name, Harry Lewis's had a slash through it.

There were a few surprises. His own mother's name was among the others. As was mine. Henry Folsom should not have been a surprise, but it was.

Noah Mosley, the richest man in town—and the one said to be the most conservative—was also there.

On one of the scraps of paper, Jeff had written: *Illegal versus immoral. Difference between the two is . . . Does it even matter? Probably not for my purposes. How much do I need? What will it take to make the bargain? How far you willing to go? She'll know if I'm just bluffing.*

On another page a note read: *KEEP KAY AWAY! Kay gets wind of any of this, she won't sit on it.*

A line from another piece of paper said: *Place to hide until I'm finished. Right under their noses.*

Jeff's wondering about a safe place to hide made me think of Miki's uncle and his men, and I stopped reading and looked around.

A car in the distance, down near where Miles Lydecker's giants had brought Lawrence Vickery, was running, the smoke of its exhaust curling up in the cold night air behind it and evaporating into the nothing above it. Its lights were off. Two men sat inside—dark figures in the darkness.

I got out of my car to have a better look around.

Why hadn't they come for Miki yet? What were they waiting for?

I thought they would've come the same night I didn't show, but now days had passed and there was still no sign of them. What was their plan? What possible advantage could they be waiting for?

I looked all around the area, keeping the car in the distance in my peripheral vision the entire time.

Eventually, the car's lights came on and it slowly drove away—past where I stood near the entrance to the USO and back down Harrison Avenue.

"How was it?" I asked.

I had Lauren safely in the car and we were headed toward the Marie Motel.

Earlier in the afternoon we had switched to the

Marie in order to be more a moving target, more elusive.

Miki was staying at Clip's tonight so Lauren and I would have the room to ourselves.

"Went well," she said.

Her voice was soft and weak, which matched her movements. It was obvious she was spent, drained, depleted.

"Are you okay?"

"Just tired."

"You're beyond tired," I said.

"Nothing being held by you and a good night's sleep can't cure."

"What all'd you do tonight?"

"Listened. Lots of listening. All any of them really want to do is talk—talk about home and their life before the war, talk about what they're doing now, what they're afraid of, what they dream of, what they want their lives to be like after the war."

"What else?"

"Talked some, of course, but not much. I mostly nod and listen."

"Did you dance?"

"Sure. Some."

I nodded, but didn't say anything.

"What is it?" she said.

"Huh?"

"What's wrong?"

"Nothing."

"Something."

"I'm tired too," I said.

"I'm sure you are. You'd have to be, but it's something else."

"It's lots of things."

"Tell me. I'm a practiced and accomplished listener."

"I'm worried about you. Think you're overdoing it."

"I am a bit. And I realize it. Gonna cut back some. I have to."

"I'm glad to hear that."

"I knew you would be. What else?"

"It's mostly that."

"Come on, Soldier. Level with me. I can take it. And you know I won't quit until you do."

"It's hard for me to think of you dancing with other men, listening for hours on end to their dreams."

"I'm sorry. I'll stop. I was just trying to find a way to help, to do something for . . . I never meant for it to bother you."

"When you respond like that," I said, "it makes me see how ridiculous and juvenile I'm being. I'm sorry."

"I think your response to the situation is typical. I'm the one—"

"I don't want to be typical."

"I meant understandable. There's nothing typical about you. And you're handling all this very well."

"I can do better."

Later that night, holding her close to me in our bed in the Marie Motel, I said, "Clip thinks maybe my issue with the money is that I think you won't need me as much, that I'm scared with more options you'll leave me eventually."

"Anything in it?" she asked.

We were spooning, my mouth at her ear, her question spoken into the darkness in front of us.

I shrugged, her body absorbing it. "I'm not sure exactly. I don't think you're with me because you lack options."

"I had money—or at least access to it—when we met."

"He reminded me of that."

"In fact, except for a very brief time recently, I've had money our entire relationship."

"I know."

She slid away slightly, turned to face me, then slid back into my embrace, our faces inches apart now.

"You're right. I'm not with you because of a lack of options. And having more options won't make me want you any less."

"I know."

"Do you? Really?"

"I do."

"Then what is it?"

"It's not just one thing."

She nodded—something I sensed more than saw.

"I want no part of anything associated with Harry or his corruption," I said. "I do have very real concerns about what money does to people. But . . . yeah . . . I guess . . . it's not that I think you want it so you'll have options or that I think you're with me now because you don't have options. But I guess I do see it as in one way or another shortening our relationship."

"I see it as just the opposite," she said. "I thought with it I might be able to get the ongoing medical treatment I need so we can prolong our time together. Make it last. Give ourselves as much time as possible. I thought if it gave us even one more day together it'd be worth all the money in the world."

She was right. I couldn't believe how stupid I had been.

I shook my head in disgust.

"How many ways can one man be wrong?" I asked.

"I'm not saying I think you are, Soldier," she said, "but if you are wrong, you are wrong for all the right reasons."

Chapter 32

"You think you righteous 'cause Clip your nigger?" Freddy said.

I didn't say anything.

We were seated in the bleachers of the Bay High School gym. I was on the third row. Sitting. Watching. Where I had been the entire time we had been here. He was on the first row, having just sat down. Towel around his shoulders. Sweat still dripping off him. Unlacing his gloves.

Gus had helped his injured sparring partner into the dressing room.

We were the only two people in the gym.

"You got no clue," he said. "You know it? No clue. Don't think you do. 'Cause you don't."

I still didn't say anything, just kept looking around the gym, watching the door.

"Just can't stand no cracker thinkin' he understand anything about us," he said. "You got no idea what it like to be us."

"Us?" I said, regretting it the moment I did.

"Negroes," he said.

I nodded, determined not to say anything else.

"And not just," he said. "Anyone who isn't like y'all. All us poor, non-white bastards that don't matter none down here under y'alls feet."

"Oh," I said. "Them."

"Not them. Us."

I nodded.

"You think 'cause Clip work for you, you ain't racist?"

"Actually, I'm workin' for him."

"You think 'cause you workin' for Clip, you ain't racist?"

"I'll give it some thought and get back to you," I said.

"I'm serious," he said. "Don't try to make a fool out of me."

"Wouldn't ever attempt to do something for you that you do so well for yourself."

"Don't think that missin' arm keep me from comin' up there and whippin' the shit out of you."

"Sparring all these bums has you thinkin' you're better than you really are," I said. "And you've forgotten that boxing isn't fighting."

"Shit man, I'd kill you without breaking a sweat."

"The problem with people like you," I said.

"People like me," he said, his voice taking on a challenging edge, his eyes narrowing beneath a deeply furrowed brow.

"Loud-mouths with a righteous cause always looking for a fight."

"Oh," he said. "So do tell me, white boy. What's the problem with people like me."

"You're right about much of what you say but you

think everything you say is right," I said. "You choose fighting as a way of life and I get it. I get why you do it. But then you don't know when not to fight, then you fight against those fighting with you."

"*You*?" he said. "You fighting *with* me? We on the same side? *Shee-it*."

"See? You can't even see it. Your justifiably angry approach has you doing the very thing you're railing against."

"Oh yeah? What's that?"

"Making assumptions. Pre-judging. Being racist."

Clip arrived to relieve me.

"You hear this shit?" Freddy said to him.

"What that?"

Freddy told him.

"Freddy, you is a dumb ass nigger. I mean, got-damn. Man is here tryin' to protect your stupid ass and you got the rocks to say he ain't fightin' with you, ain't on your side?"

"You really think he take a bullet for me?" Freddy said.

Clip shook his head in frustration and disgust.

"You need to think long and hard about what I doin' for you, for all us, 'fore you be callin' me a dumb nigger," Freddy said.

"Jimmy here already done far more for me than you ever could," Clip said. "Damn site more than what your running your mouth in the paper ever gonna do."

"What happen when I beat the bum?" Freddy said. "What you say then? I win the fight, my words take on more weight. People listen. And I ain't afraid to say what need to be said. You gonna show me some goddamn respect then, ain't you boy?"

Clip didn't even acknowledge anything had been said.

"Can't believe your Uncle Tom ass gonna side with this cracker ass motherfucker," Freddy said. "One of them. A member of the very machine we bein' flattened by."

"What was it tipped you off?" Clip asked. "The way he dress? The work he do? Who he work for? Who he associate with?"

"He married to money."

"He ain't married to nobody," Clip said. "That alone show he ain't a cog in the machine. And if who he with happen to have some money, fact that he still here doin' this say even more about him. But more than that, it say the most about you. Your puppet ass ain't had an original thought and you too blind to see what really goin' on around you. You just parroting shit you heard somebody else say. Ain't thinkin' for yourself. Ain't speaking for yourself. But no matter who got they hand up your ass or pullin' your strings, you say some shit like this again, and we walk. We let whoever want to kill your dumb ass do it. Hell, may even help 'em."

Lady Bird Bennett not only opened her enormous solid wood door for Henry Folsom, she welcomed us inside as well.

"So good of you to come," she said, as she ushered us in. "I'm sorry the house is such a mess, but I've been so devastated I've been unable to do anything at all."

Of the many things wrong with what she had said, two in particular stood out most prominently. The house was truly and exquisitely immaculate. And whatever cleaning needed doing and whenever it needed doing, it wouldn't be the lady Bird of the house doing it.

"Noah and I were just about to have some tea," she said. "Would you gentleman please join us?"

She led us through the house and out onto the back porch overlooking the bay where Noah Mosley sat in a three-piece suit sipping tea and enjoying one of the best views in town.

He was a tall, large older man whose dramatic features had only become more exaggerated with age—elongated ears, enormous nose, and huge teeth in a slightly misshapen mouth.

"Henry," he said, standing and extending his hand enthusiastically.

Nothing about the ravages of time or the toll taken on his body had diminished the dignity with which Noah Mosley comported himself. He had money. He had power. He mattered. No one else did—or at least not nearly as much.

"Noah," Folsom said, shaking his hand. "How are you?"

"Never better."

"This is Jimmy Riley. Don't know if you two've met."

"Heard of him, but we haven't met," Noah said, and there was something in the way he said it, a subtle but undeniable something—some knowledge he believed he possessed, some scrap of information he could disapprove of.

"I know of him through Harry Lewis," he said to Folsom, never actually looking at me.

He shook my left hand awkwardly with his right—making a point to point out just how awkward it was—quickly, dismissively, then returned to his seat.

Lady Bird's maid appeared and poured our tea and served our scones.

"Do you have news about who killed my Jeffrey?"

"We do need to talk to you about that," Folsom said, cutting his eyes quickly over to Mosley then back.

"Noah is my closest adviser, Henry," she said. "You know that. You can say anything in front of him. Anything. And I insist you do. Be just as candid as you would've been had it been just me."

"Well, it's just . . . there's some question about the

identification."

"Identification?"

"Of the body."

"What body?"

"The one you identified as your son."

"I don't understand."

"We have another identification that—"

"Another? Of Jeffrey? Why? Who?"

"She says it's not him," he said. "That she's certain of it."

"*She*?" Lady Bird said, her voice conveying more outrage and incredulity than seemed possible to fit into one syllable. "*Certain*?"

Folsom waited.

"Henry, I'm sure you can imagine but this is hard enough without the added . . . absurdity of someone saying I don't know my own son. Who would do such a— It's that horrible home wrecker, isn't it? Hudson."

"She was with him recently," Folsom said. "Says she's certain it's not him. Mentioned a recent wound he got overseas."

"I'm sure I don't know what she's playing at, but I'm surprised you could be so gullible. For Christ's sake, Henry. I know you're upset about Gladys. I know you've been shot and haven't recovered, but this is just too much. It really is."

"We had to check," he said. "Had to hear you say you were certain. Had to make sure that in your grief and . . . that you didn't make a mistake."

"A mistake? A *mistake*?"

"I'm sorry," he said. "But we had to hear you say it."

"Well," Noah Mosley said, "and now you have. I'll see you out."

He stood. Folsom followed.

I waited.

"Why would she lie?" I said. "What's she playing at?"

"I'm sure I can't imagine," she said.

Mosley and Folsom had taken a few steps out of the room and now had returned.

"Rebecca could confirm the identification," I said. "Still no word from her?"

"My identification of my son needs no confirmation," she said.

"I'll see you out, Mr. Riley," Mosley said.

"You still want me to find her, right?" I said. "Where was she last seen?"

"Her brother lives in Port St. Joe," she said. "She may have gone there. If I knew, I wouldn't have hired you. A decision I'm beginning to have serious doubts about."

"Time to go," Mosley said.

"Let's go, Jimmy," Folsom said, touching my shoulder.

I stood.

"We're very sorry to have had to disturb you like this," Folsom said to Bennett.

"I know you're just doing your job, Henry," she said. "I understand. I do. It's just a tough time."

"Could you possibly be any more deferential, Henry?" I said.

We were in the driveway, walking toward the car.

"You don't think I handled that the right way?" he said. "What would you have me do, Jimmy? It's not like we know for sure which one of them is lying."

"You're awfully close with them," I said.

"No, I'm not. It's something they do. The rich are different. They act different. They act as if every public servant is a close friend."

When we reached the car, we didn't get in, just stood on either side of it, talking to each other over the roof.

"I'm not talking about how *they* acted," I said.

"I play along somewhat," he said. "I have to. Goes with the territory."

"What else does?"

"Whatta you mean?"

"What else goes with that territory?"

"That's it."

"Come on, Henry," I said. "You're in their pocket."

"I'm not in anybody's pocket."

"Don't forget who you're talkin' to," I said.

"In my entire career—hell, in my entire life—I made one deal with the devil. I did it for Gladys. I had to. Never before. Never again. The end."

"Your name is on a list of people that includes theirs," I said, jerking my head back toward Lady Bird's house.

"What kind of list?"

"One Jeff Bennett made before he disappeared. Lee Perkins was on it too. Bennett was working on a story about local war profiteering and the black market in this area. What are y'all up to?"

He frowned and shook his head. "I'm not up to anything. Not with them or anyone else. All I'm doing is my damn job. I'm a good cop. I've done a lot of good over the years—and it's been a lot of years. I do one bad thing for a good reason and suddenly I'm corrupt, I'm . . . like them? Let me ask you something. What if you were judged not for decades of good, not for millions of good things, but for one bad thing?"

"Well, as bad things go it was a doozie," I said. "But that's the thing, boss—no way to know that it was just the one thing. No way to ever be sure again."

"So the fact that you backshot a man . . ."

"Means I'm capable of it," I said. "Means you can never know for sure that I won't do it again."

He frowned and shook his head again and we got into the car.

"But two things—" I said as he cranked the car and began backing down the drive. "It was two men, not one. And comparing backshooting two career criminals to save Lauren with taking money from a black market bastard profiting on the wartime sacrifices of others, helping two sick fuck sadists torture and murder young women, and helping them try to do the same to Lauren and to kill me is a bit of a stretch, even for a corrupt cop like you."

Chapter 34

I was alone in my office looking over Jeff's notes again when our old secretary July opened the door and strolled in just like she used to.

"Got a minute?" she said, sitting down across from me without waiting for my reply.

The last time I had seen her, she had been on this side of the desk, her dead body splayed in my chair.

"I've missed you," I said.

"You think you're dreaming, don't you, fella?" she said.

I shook my head. "Pretty sure I'm awake."

"Then how do you explain this?"

"Don't plan to."

"Not even to yourself?" she asked.

"Especially not to myself."

"You're not curious?" she said. "You've got to be. You are about everything."

"Not everything. Only those things that might actually have an explanation."

She nodded appreciatively. "God, I've missed you."

We were silent a moment.

"Looks like you've missed me more," she added. "You don't look so good, Soldier."

"Been worse."

"Before Lauren," she said. "Before you got her back."

I nodded, but there was no need. She was making statements, not asking questions.

"Do anything to keep her, wouldn't you?" she said.

"I think you know the answer to that," I said.

"I need to ask you something, Soldier," she said. "Need your advice. What do you do when you need to tell someone you care about something they don't want to hear?"

I shrugged. "Depends."

"On?"

I heard a creak on the staircase.

Someone was coming up to my office.

I pulled open the top left drawer of my desk and put my hand on the .38 that was there, even though I had been carrying one in a shoulder holster beneath what remained of my right arm since Miki's uncle had issued his ultimatum.

"Come over here behind me in case—" I started saying to July, but when I looked up from the drawer, she was gone.

It sounded as if the person was trying to be quiet, but there was also a certain labored awkwardness that made that an impossibility.

Was it two people? A heavy person? And then it hit me. It was the soft, injury-awkward steps of David Howell.

"Don't shoot, it's me," he yelled when he neared the top of the stairs.

It took him a little while, but eventually he made it to the top of the steps, across the outer office, and into one of the same chairs across from my desk July had just been sitting in.

"You think we can talk to the dead?" I said.

His eyes widened. "You okay there, fella?"

"Not sure exactly. Doesn't matter. Been a while. Where you been?"

"Around," he said. "In the shadows. Keeping an eye on you."

"What's it like watching a master?" I said. "Pick up any new detecting skills?"

"Really surprised there's been no Jap attack yet," he said. "Wonder what he's playin' at?"

"Wish I knew," I said. "I'm carrying around some major tension in my shoulders I'd love to get rid of. He's far more patient and calculating than I would've thought."

"Is it possible it was just a hollow threat?"

I shook my head. "Don't think so. Miki says not."

He nodded and seemed to mull it over.

"Know anything about Noah Mosley?" I asked.

He shook his head. "Not much. I've seen him in Folsom's office a few times. Hell, see him everywhere. Owns half the town, doesn't he? Why?"

"He was with Lady Bird Bennett when we went to talk to her this morning. His name's on a list of corrupt people and war profiteers in Jeff's notes."

"Oh yeah?"

"Folsom's on the list too."

He looked genuinely shocked.

"No way he's profiting off the war," he said. "No way."

When I didn't agree right away, his eyebrows shot up.

"Something you need to tell me?" he said.

"I'm not saying he's a war profiteer," I said. "I seriously doubt he is. But I'm not certain he's not compromised. I don't know. Think maybe he's keeping the wrong company, closing his eyes to corruption if not participating in it directly."

He thought about it.

"You know more than you're saying," he said.

"Maybe, but not much."

"Level with me, fella," he said. "Soldier to soldier."

"I know for sure of only one thing he did," I said. "Said he did it for very personal reasons, which I believe. Said it was only the once, which I'm not as convinced of."

"What'd he do?"

"It was what he didn't do," I said.

He nodded. "That's all I'm gettin', isn't it?"

I nodded.

"Okay, Soldier. Thanks for the trust."

He was right. I was trusting him some. Not much, but as far as it went, it was more than any other cop I was dealing with at the moment.

"I got info of my own to share," he said. "Why I'm here."

"Let's have it."

"Got an ID on the body."

"Yeah?"

"Yeah," he said. "Whatta you think? Bennett or not?"

I thought about it. "Have no idea, but my guess, my gut, is not Bennett."

"Give your gut its due," he said. "It's right. Victim's

name is Cecil Deets."

"What's his story?"

"Thought we'd go find out."

As we descended the stairs, Kay Hudson opened the door and started up them.

When she saw us, she turned instead, went back outside, and was waiting for us on the sidewalk when we emerged from the boarded-up doorway of the shot-up building.

"Where are you two off to in such a hurry?"

I had to suppress a laugh so as not to make David feel self-conscious. There was nothing fast about the way we were moving.

I told her what we were up to.

"I told you," she said. "She's a conniving, lying . . . Now do you believe me?"

"About?"

"Everything."

"I believe you about the ID," I said. "And that goes a long way toward giving credibility to the other things you've told me, but you're not telling me everything."

"Who was it?" she asked. "If not Jeff, then who?"

"We shouldn't say yet," David said.

She looked at me. "Seems the least you could do for me. Besides, if he's a friend of Jeff's, I may know him."

"Cecil Deets," I said.

She looked blankly.

"Don't know him?" I asked.

She shook her head. "Don't think so."

"Works at the Bird of Paradise," I said. "We're

headed over there right now."

"It's possible his death has nothing to do with Jeff," David said. "Just a misidentification. You sure you don't know of any connection between them?"

"I don't," she said.

"Co you can't think of any reason Jeff would have to want to hurt or kill him?"

"Absolutely none at all," she said. "Would never happen. Not in a million years. There's probably no connection whatsoever to Jeff, but if there is it's not because Jeff killed him. I'd stake my life on it."

"Okay," I said. "Thanks. I'll keep you—"

"I'm going with you," she said.

"No you're not," David said. "You can't."

"Of course I can and I am. Not only is Mr. Riley in my employ, but I'm a member of the press and we can go anywhere."

The Bird of Paradise was Panama City's only queer club.

It was an old, small fishing shack on the end of a dock out in Massalina Bayou.

Very, very few people knew about it—which was how it remained in existence. That and the fact that the owner Thomas Queen—his real name—guarded what went on in the joint like it was all he had in the entire world.

A large, iridescent Ribbon-tailed Astrapia was painted on the front slat-board wall, its huge head and neck shimmering, glittering green and gold and blue, its full body a rainbow of brilliant colors on the tips of shiny black feathers.

"Think I'll wait out here," Howell said.

"Yeah?" I asked.

"Yeah."

I started to ask why but decided it could wait.

Kay and I walked the rest of the way down the narrow dock and inside the leaning building.

We found Tommy Q working behind the bar. It was midafternoon and the small shack was mostly empty.

An older woman sat at the end of the bar nursing a

bottle of beer, and a couple of youngish guys sat at a table in the back corner sipping something colorful from large martini glasses. Otherwise it was just us.

"As I live and breathe," Tommy said when he saw me. "Jimmy fuckin' Riley. It's been a while, baby."

His voice was deep and smoky, but soft and sensual too. Next to his deeply tanned skin, his bright white teeth and silver eyes shone brilliantly—the latter matching his coarse, closely cropped hair.

"You two know each other?" Kay asked in surprise.

"Not just each other," Tommy said. "We know everybody in this tiny town—well, at least all those worth knowing."

She looked at me. "Just keep the surprises coming, Soldier. I don't mind."

"Soldier here and I have fought a few wars together," Tommy said.

"Don't believe him," I said. "Him saving my ass is not the same as us fighting together."

"It's a fine ass," he said. "Worth saving. But don't be so damn modest. You saved this ol' girl's ass a time or three also."

I hadn't realized until that moment that I had picked up the phrase *a time or three* from him.

We each took a seat at the bar.

"I know what you want," he said to me. "What would the lady like?"

She told him and he began pouring and mixing our drinks.

"Are you . . ." Kay began.

"Is he what?" Tommy said. "A fruit? Really? Come on. It's a pity, but you can smell the straight on him."

"I misjudged you Jimmy Riley," she said.

"Why should you be any different?" Tommy said. "We all do it to everybody all the time."

When he finished the drinks and set them on the bar, there were three. Lifting his, he said, "To peace."

"To peace," we said, and all touched glasses.

We each enjoyed our drinks in silence for a moment.

"I'm afraid I've got some very bad news," I said.

He frowned. "Cecil?" he asked.

I nodded.

"How'd you know?" Kay asked.

"He's been missing for a few days," he said. "And that was the worst news I could think of."

"I'm so sorry," she said.

Tommy quickly drank the rest of his drink and poured another. "Gonna need a few of these. To Cecil."

"To Cecil," we both said, and clinked glass again.

"What happened?" he asked.

"That's what we're trying to find out," I said, and told him what we knew.

He took another drink. As he did, his attention drifted over to the two guys at the table in the corner, his eyebrows rising as he did.

I followed his gaze. The two guys had abandoned their drinks in what looked like an attempt to drink each other.

"Hey," he said. "You two need to go get a room somewhere. You passed the point of how far you can go in here a mile or so back. Not gonna get closed down over you two creamin' your little panties."

"Sorry, Tommy Q," one of the guys said.

"Just got carried away. We wouldn't want to get our

favorite place shut down."

"Yeah, yeah," he said, then returned his attention to our drinks.

He filled his up again. Noticed ours were empty, and refilled them too.

Lifting his glass, he said, "To catching the bastard that killed that sweet boy."

We all drank to that.

"Any ideas who that might be?" I asked.

"Everybody loved Cecil D," he said. "Such a sweet kid. Gotta be some queer basher."

"Any idea why he would be at a room in the Dixie?" I asked.

"I'm sure doing what those two want to be doing right now," he said, nodding toward the two in the corner. "He'd sometimes meet men here and go back to their room with 'em. Could've gone with the wrong one or ran into someone there who realized what he was. Just do me a favor."

"What's that?"

"You find the fuck, you give me a little time alone with him before you do anything else. He wants to tussle with a queer, this ol' queen'll give him a go."

I nodded.

"Pickin' on poor, sweet Cecil. I'll show him just how butch some bitches can get."

"I'll see what I can do," I said.

"Thank you, baby."

"Do you know of any connection between Cecil and Jeff Bennett?" I asked.

"The boxer?"

"Yeah."

"No. Why?"

"Ever seen him in here?"

"No way. Never. Did he kill Cecil? Was he beaten to death?"

"No," Kay said. "No way."

"He's missing and some people misidentified Cecil as Jeff at first. Did Cecil steal?"

"A bit, yeah. Nothing major, but you had to watch your things when he was around. You think that has something to do with—"

"I'm asking because I don't know," I said. "Don't know anything yet. Not really."

"I know you. It won't stay that way long," he said. "Not long at all."

Chapter 36

"How'd it go?" David asked.

"Didn't learn a lot," I said, "but got a little info."

"And had some drinks," he said.

"A couple," Kay said. "You missed out."

"Why didn't you go in?" I asked.

"I'll be honest, it was partly my . . . discomfort, but mostly . . . I didn't want to see anything I'd have to arrest anyone for."

"You're all right," I said. "You're all right."

"Turns out ol' Jimmy here is good pals with the owner," Kay said.

"Hope that doesn't mean you have to arrest me."

"There's a story there," Kay said. "I want to hear it."

I nodded.

"Seriously," she said. "How the hell does a one-armed private detective who's so straight you can smell it on him become friends with a queer?"

"Is that what he is?" I asked. "Is that all he is?"

"Is it just him or all queers?" she said.

"Is what?"

"I just can't get over . . . I'm just very surprised.

That's all. Things I've seen all over the world, not much surprises me. You do."

"Okay," David said, "besides having drinks and finding out that Soldier here consorts with known sodomites, anything else y'all care to share? You know, about the case?"

I told him what Tommy told us about Cecil.

"You believe him?" he asked.

I nodded. "Every word."

"So we find who he went to the Dixie with and who he encountered there," he said.

I nodded.

"Are we thinking most likely scenario is that Jeff Bennett killed him and is on the run?"

"I'm certainly not," Kay said. "There's no way that happened. No possible way."

"Is Jeff Bennett a fruit?" David asked her.

"Be sure to ask him when you find him," she said. "I saw him knock a guy's two front teeth out for less. Oh, and be sure to use a word like *sodomite*."

He shook his head. "I'm going to the Dixie to see what I can find out. Check in with you later."

I nodded.

"Want a ride back to your office?" he asked.

"We'll walk. Thanks."

"What the hell was all that about?" I asked.

Kay Hudson and I were walking down Beach toward Harrison, Massalina Bayou on our right, St. Andrew Bay on our left.

"What?"

"Why go on and on about—"

"Bothered Howell, didn't it?" she said.

"Think that's smart? He's the cop trying to help find your friend."

"He actually said *known sodomite*."

"I think he was being facetious," I said.

"I didn't get that. Hope he was. Hope I just missed it."

We crossed over the bridge and continued down the other side.

"Queers really don't bother you?" she said.

"Bother me?"

"You know what I'm asking," she said. "How can you be okay with . . . You're a straight white man in the South. You're part of the power, you—"

"Black man said the same thing to me this morning."

"And?"

"I'm not."

"You're not what?"

"Part of any power anything," I said.

"But I'm asking how you're not, how you're so . . ."

"Why does it matter?"

"It just does."

"Do you want to fire me?"

She stopped.

"*Fire you?*" she said, her voice rising. "I want to hug you."

And then she did.

We were standing at the corner of Beach and Harrison, her embracing me enthusiastically.

"I just hired you because you were the only PI in town," she said. "I had no way of knowing you were . . .

the way you are. I couldn't be completely honest with you before."

"But you can now?"

"I can."

"Let's have it."

"Here? Now?"

"Right here. Right now."

She looked around us. There were cars and pedestrians all about, but no one near enough to hear us.

"Jeff and Becky," she said, "have a marriage of convenience. Don't get me wrong, they care deeply for one another and do great work together. But they don't have a conventional marriage."

I waited.

She studied my reaction, then continued.

"They each have other relationships . . . other lovers . . . of the same sex."

"Okay," I said.

"I'm Becky's."

"So she's who you really want to find?" I asked.

"I want to find them both, but . . . yeah, she's my main motivation."

I nodded. "I understand why you couldn't tell me," I said. "Anything else you've been keeping from me?"

"Just that that bitch Birdie Bennett is behind all this. She knows what her son is but won't accept it, won't even admit it. She's determined to change him by any means. She's crazy. She's . . ."

"Homicidal?"

"There's no question she's behind Cecil's death," she said. "None. She'd never do it herself, but make no mistake about it, she had it done. Think about it—who lies about her own son being dead? Actually misidentifies the body? Wherever she has them, whatever she's doing with them, they're in real danger."

Chapter 37

I pressed the small barrel of the .38 into the back of Lawrence Vickery's head.

He lifted his arms, holding his greasy hands out.

He had been working on Lady Bird's car when I came up behind him, and I had wondered if he had a wrench or screwdriver in his hand he might use for a weapon.

"Come on," I said. "We're going for a ride."

"Okay, take it easy, pal. Where we going?"

"You're gonna take me where you took Jeff and Rebecca," I said.

"And if I refuse? What then?"

"Depends," I said, "but it'll be between a bullet to your small brain, having a chat with your employer, or turning you over to Miles Lydecker. Or maybe all three—though I'm not sure what order. I'll just have to improvise that."

"Okay. Okay. Let's go for a ride, fella, but I'll tell you this—I doubt I can find the place again. What if I can't? What happens then?"

"We've already covered that," I said.

"He needs help," Vickery said. "Why don't y'all just leave him where he is."

He was driving. I was in the seat behind him with the gun pressed to the back of his head. Kay Hudson was in the passenger seat with a gun of her own. And having insisted on coming, Lauren was in the seat beside me.

We were heading west on 98 along the coast toward Fort Walton.

The night was darkish, the moon shrouded in clouds, our half headlights having difficulty penetrating the fog.

"Help with what?" Kay asked.

"His perversion."

"Hear that Jimmy?" Kay said. "The gambling chauffeur knows more than he let on."

"What perversion?" Lauren asked. "What's he talking about?"

"He's a deviant," Vickery said.

"You don't know?" Kay asked Lauren in surprise, turning slightly in the seat to see her.

"Know what?"

"Do you two share the same views?" Kay asked.

Lauren laughed. "On what? We see money a little differently."

I smiled.

"We share the same views on most things," Lauren said.

"On everything that matters," I said.

"Not that any of it matters," Lauren said.

"Surely everything matters," Kay said.

"You're right," she said. "It does."

"And yet it doesn't," I said. "Only one thing really matters."

Lauren nodded. "Exactly. And that one thing is everything."

"And that is?"

"Lauren," I said, as she was saying, "Jimmy."

Kay smiled. "That's sweet."

"It's not," I said. "It's not sweet or sentimental or— We've been through hell, and what we have has cost us so much."

"Cost us everything," Lauren said.

"Didn't mean to diminish it in any way," Kay said. "Honestly. I get it. I have that same kind of love with . . . my . . ."

We all fell silent a few beats.

I wanted so badly to take Lauren's hand. I never missed having two hands more than in moments like these.

"What I wanted to ask was . . . Is there any sort of person you wouldn't want him helping?" Kay asked Lauren.

"Sure," she said. "Nazis. Brutes. Anybody who would hurt a child or a woman."

"Just come out and ask her what you want to," I said.

Kay looked at me. "Do you know where she stands on the subject? Have you two ever spoken about it?"

I shook my head.

"Gentleman Jeff Bennett is a queer," Vickery blurted out. "That's what she's trying to tell you. Your husband's helping a fruit. 'Course maybe he's a little fruity too. Maybe you already know that."

Lauren smiled a little and looked at me.

"Do you mind?" Kay asked.

"Of course I mind," Lauren said.

We all looked at her a little more intently.

"See?" Vickery said. "I ain't the only normal person in this car."

"You do?" Kay asked her.

"If you're talking about the driver's rude behavior," Lauren said. "I mind it a great deal."

I tapped Vickery's head with the barrel of the revolver.

"If you're talking about who people love and how they love and what they love," Lauren said, "then of course I don't mind. Can't help who you love. No one should try to stop you."

"Jesus Christ," Vickery said.

"I spoke with a very scared young man earlier in the week," Lauren said. "He's terrified he'll be found out. The way we're treating those willing to fight and die for our country is truly dreadful. Have you heard about this?"

Kay nodded. "We didn't even have a policy of keeping homosexuals out of the military before the war began. Now we've got all sorts of screenings. Directives coming down from on high. We've got psychiatrists using words like *sexual psychopathy*."

"His cousin was killed at Pearl Harbor and since that moment all he's wanted to do was avenge his death, fight for his country. He just knew the doctor interviewing him was going to know exactly what he is. But all he asked him was did he like girls, and he answered honestly yes, of course he likes girls. He likes them a lot—as friends and confidants, just not sexual partners."

I thought about the good Lauren had been doing at the USO, thought about how I had behaved, what I had said and mostly what I had thought, and felt ashamed.

"What I was saying earlier," Kay said, "and feared to finish was that Becky and I have the same kind of love you two do."

"I don't doubt it," Lauren said.

"We just live in a world where we're not allowed to have it—or at least not let on that we have it."

"The world doesn't exactly sanction our love either," Lauren said. "I was married when we met. Now . . . we're together, live together, and aren't married."

"Why aren't you two married?" Kay asked. "Unlike us you can be."

"What we have is so far beyond . . ." Lauren began. "It seems, at least to me, that getting married at this point would lessen it somehow. But that's just how I see it. You'll have to ask Jimmy why he hasn't asked me to."

Chapter 38

"We're here," Vickery said.

Here was a dirt road off Highway 98 between Panama City Beach and Destin—not nearly as far west and into Fort Walton as Vickery had originally claimed.

At the end of the straight, narrow road, an old, smallish two-story converted hotel sat next to a body of water I didn't recognize. A lake perhaps. It was difficult to tell in the darkness, though the moon had come partially out from behind the clouds and glowed eerily on the smooth surface of the water.

The area was unpopulated and densely forested—consisting primarily of sand hills, wet flatwoods, and prairies and cypress swamps.

The night noises, all the chirps and croaks, squeaks and nocturnal songs, were louder than anything that could be heard back in Panama City—even among the all-night activities on Harrison.

A sign near the building read Point Washington Center for Reparative Therapy and Treatment.

"Oh my God," Kay Hudson said.

"What is it?" Lauren asked.

"It's one of those places."

"'Those places'?" I asked.

"A torture chamber of barbaric horrors. They do aversion therapy for the prevention and elimination of homosexual behavior. We're talking electrodes to the genitals. We're talking the most inhumane, violent, harmful brutality you can imagine. Torture drugs. Shock therapy. Even ice pic lobotomies and castrations."

"Is an ice pic lobotomy what it sounds like?" Lauren asked.

"Transorbital lobotomy, where the so-called surgeon enters the prefrontal area of the brain through the patient's eye sockets with an instrument resembling—or in some cases an actual—household ice pic."

"This is where you brought them?" I asked Vickery. "You're sure?"

"*Them*?" Kay said. "I thought it was only Jeff. Becky is here too?"

Without waiting for a reply, she jumped out of the car and ran across the yard, up the stairs, and into the building.

"Come on," I said to Vickery. "Help us in here and you live. Do anything other than that or if anything goes wrong, you're the first one to die tonight. Understand?"

He nodded.

I handed Lauren a gun, kissed her, and Vickery and I followed Kay.

Inside, the place was dim and quiet.

There was no one in the lobby or at the front desk.

I shoved Vickery past the desk, toward the hallways and stairs in the back.

When we reached the corridors, we peered down

both. No movement. No light. Nothing.

The ceiling above us shook, and we could hear running coming from the hallway upstairs.

"Upstairs," I yelled. "Now."

He opened the stairwell door and ran up the two flights of stairs, me following close behind him.

"Don't trip and shoot me," he said.

When we reached the top floor, we found Kay Hudson pointing a gun at a red-headed, freckled young orderly, who was leading her from room to room.

"There are only three others," he said.

"Show me," she said.

"Why're you doing this?" he asked. "You really need to talk to Dr. Delpy. May I call him in for you?"

"No you may not. You may find me the people I'm looking for."

He opened the next door, turned on the light, and they disappeared inside.

Vickery and I waited in the hall.

Emerging a few moments later, Kay shook her head.

A moment after they entered the next room, I heard her exclaim, "Jeff! Oh, thank God. Jeff. Jeff? Jeff? It's me, Kay. Jeff? What's wrong?"

We went inside to find a poor, confused creature who bore very little resemblance to the legendary boxing war correspondent Gentleman Jeff Bennett.

Kay looked at the orderly.

"He's still recovering from the procedure Dr. Delpy performed on him. He'll still get some better."

"Some? *Some*?"

"He won't be a sexual deviant anymore."

"Help him up," I said to Vickery. "Let's get him out

of here."

"Come on," Kay said, motioning to the orderly with her gun.

Vickery helped Jeff up as the orderly led Kay into the next room.

When we were back out in the hall, I heard Kay say, "Who's this? This isn't—"

"Whatta you want me to do with him?" Vickery asked, holding Jeff by the arm.

"Walk him up and down the hallway. Try to get him to wake up."

"It ain't that he's asleep," Vickery said.

Kay and the orderly stepped back into the hallway.

"Where is she?" Kay asked.

"Who?" the orderly said. "That's everyone. We have no female patients at the moment."

"Rebecca Bennett," she said. "His wife. Where is she?"

"She didn't survive the procedure," he said. "It happens sometimes."

Kay's knees buckled and she fell back against the wall.

"Dr. Delpy's success rate is very high," the orderly was saying, "but . . . occasionally you get one that doesn't respond well to the treatment plan."

"Shut up," Kay yelled. "Stop talking."

Pushing herself off the wall, she brought the barrel of the small revolver to the bridge of the orderly's nose.

"Where is she?"

"It just happened. Earlier this evening. The body's in a room downstairs until the funeral home can pick it up in the morning."

"It?"

"Give me the gun, Kay," I said.

"Show me," she said. "Show *it* to me."

"I didn't mean anything by it. I just meant—"

"Say another word and *you'll* be an *it*," she said. "Show me."

He led her back down the stairs, Vickery, Jeff, and I following close behind.

When we reached the lobby, I said to Vickery, "Stand here with Jeff so I can see you. If you move, you die."

He did as he was told, and I walked down the corridor behind Kay, to the second door on the right, and to her fate awaiting behind it.

This time when Kay's knees gave way there was no wall to catch her, and she fell to the floor sobbing.

Rebecca Bennett was laid out, her nude body only partially covered by the white sheet, her beautiful brown hair splayed out around her face, her skin pale as moonlight on river water, the corners of each eye still seeping blood.

Kay tried to stand but was unable.

I reached down and helped pull her up the best I could.

Once on her feet again she stumbled over and fell onto her lover, draping her upper body over the breasts that, like Lauren's were for me, must once have been her safe place of refuge from the tumult and tempest of life.

Above her, Becky wept tears of blood, crimson rivulets trickling down death-pale skin not yet gone waxy.

And I cried tears of my own.

Chapter 39

A very long while later, Kay, Lauren, and I stood in the lobby.

"I'll let you decide what we do next," I said to Kay. "I can call David or Folsom, have them come over. We can call the locals or—"

"Help me get everybody out," she said. "I'm gonna burn it to the ground. I don't care who you call after that."

Lauren nodded. "We can do that," she said.

Torching the place would make it all the more difficult to prosecute and convict Delpy and those behind this, but . . . since it wasn't all that likely to happen anyway—particularly if Birdie Bennett and Noah Mosley were involved—and since I knew firsthand exactly what she was going through, knew how much she needed to burn something, anything, the whole world if possible, I agreed to it.

In short order, I called David Howell and Henry Folsom, and we evacuated the building, Kay insisting on carrying Becky on her own, and using gas we siphoned from our car and that of the orderly's, we set a fire Prometheus would be proud of.

By the time Folsom and Howell arrived, there was very little left of the structure, and everything there was, was engulfed in flames.

"What the hell happened?" Folsom said.

"You need to find Dr. Delpy," I said. "It's his place. The orderly should be helpful with that. Just threaten him a little. Delpy's a quack trying to cure homosexuality with electric shock to the genitals and ice pics to the brain. He's killed one of his patients that we know of. I'm sure there are others."

The three of us were standing away from everyone else.

"How'd the fire start?" Folsom asked.

I shrugged. "It's an old tinderbox. No telling how long it's been here. Maybe Delpy did it to destroy evidence. Thankfully we got everybody out."

"How'd you find this place?" David asked.

"Lady Bird Bennett's chauffeur," I said. "He brought us out."

"And you didn't think you should let us know?"

"I did. It's why you're standing here," I said. "The moment there was something to tell, I told it. And I didn't tell it to just anybody. I told it to you two."

"Okay. Okay. Don't get worked up," David said.

"She's behind all this," I said.

"Who?" Folsom asked, looking over his shoulder toward the cars and the people standing there with Kay and Lauren.

"Bennett," I said. "It's why she lied about her son being dead. She had him brought here for this barbaric treatment. She's responsible for all the death and destruction. I don't think her son will ever be right again."

"Not like he was right to begin with," Folsom said.

"Tell me you're gonna do the right thing," I said. "That you're not going to let her pay you off."

"Nobody's payin' me off anything," he said. "I'll get everyone responsible for this. Everyone."

"I'm not talking about everyone," I said. "I'm talking about the main one. Your good friend, the mother of the city you work for."

"Everyone," he said.

"You heard that," I said to Howell.

He didn't say anything, just gave me the slightest of nods.

"I've reached my limit of letting you accuse me of being corrupt," Folsom said.

"I've reached a few limits of my own," I said. "You've gotten away with some shit before because there was nothing legally I could do about it. That won't happen again. If you don't do what's right here, if you let your personal distaste or Birdie Bennett's money keep you from doing what you know is right, I will burn your life to the ground."

"You're tired, upset, injured," he said. "So I'm gonna let you threatening a police officer slide, but just this once. Last chance, kid. Better use it wisely."

He turned to David.

"Get him the hell out of here before I do something I can't undo."

"What's wrong with the world?" Lauren asked.

We were holding each other beneath the covers in our warm bed in the Dixie Sherman hotel, after having made love.

We had moved once again. This time out of the Marie and back to the Dixie.

We had come in spent and smelling of smoke, but too grateful to be together not to express how we felt—to one another, to the world.

"Nothing right now," I said.

"I know. And that makes me feel so guilty. I keep imagining Kay Hudson all alone in her bed, or Jeff drooling in his, and I feel so bad for them."

I nodded. "Me too."

In actuality, Jeff was in a hospital bed under a different name, Kay in a chair beside him, but it made me feel no less bad for them both.

"What they were doing at that place was not too unlike what they say the Nazis are doing."

I nodded.

"In our own backyard."

"I know."

"It's too much."

"It is."

"What're we gonna do?"

"Keep loving each other," I said. "Keep fighting back the forces of evil. You'll keep helping Gladys and the soldiers at the USO. I'll keep bumblin' around in the dark trying to shine a light. But for now . . . we'll sleep."

Chapter 40

When I arrived at the gym the next morning, I found Clip in the ring working with Gus, Freddy's trainer.

He was wearing Freddy's gear, and except for the gauntness and eyepatch, he looked remarkably like him.

I walked over and sat down on the first row of bleachers beside Saul.

"Jimmy," he said.

"What's going on?"

"Freddy's gone," he said.

"Where?"

"Just gone. Decided to run. Left a note. Left town."

"What's Clip doin'?"

"Says he's gonna fight in Freddy's place."

"What?"

"Told me to put in the paper that Freddy has lost a lot of weight and injured his eye during training but that the fight would still go on."

"He'll get killed," I said. "Lights Out is too good a boxer for a skinny, one-eyed guy with no experience with boxing."

"He'd get killed if he had two eyes," Saul said. "As it

is . . ."

"Now," I said, "if it was a street fight . . ."

"But it ain't," he said. "And the ref ain't gonna let it turn into that. You gotta talk to him."

"What'd Freddy's note say?"

"Threat of death was too much. That he couldn't take Lydecker pressuring him no more. That there was no way to pay him back and his pride wouldn't let him take a dive."

"Somethin' I gots to do," Clip said.

"Why?"

He was still inside the ring, still had his gloves on. I was standing outside the ropes near one of the corners. Gus, who was giving us a minute, was over talking to Saul.

"Think 'bout all he done said in the paper," he said. "Not just what he said, but the way he said it."

"Yeah?"

"He stood up. Spoke truth. He full of himself, full of shit, but . . . he said a lot needed sayin'."

I nodded.

"How it gonna look he run away like a coward?"

"Doesn't change the truth he spoke," I said.

"Does for anybody wantin' it not to be true," he said. "He don't fight, it not just reflect on him."

He was right.

"But . . . the fight's in two days," I said. "Against one of the top heavyweights in the world."

"I know. And you keepin' me from trainin'."

"You could get seriously injured," I said. "Or worse."

"I know."

"What he said or how it looks if he doesn't fight isn't worth that," I said.

"I think it is."

"You're willin' to die for another man's words?" I asked.

"Lots a people do that," he said. "But they was my words. Least most of 'em."

"What?"

"I tol' him what to say."

I was more surprised than I should've been.

"Freddy ain't a big thinker," he said. "He had a audience but nothin' to say."

"So you coached him on what to say."

"Not his words I willin' to die for," he said. "It mine."

Chapter 41

When I walked out of the Bay High School gym, Miki's uncle and his two young gunsels were waiting for me.

One in front. One behind. Both jabbing barrels at me as the uncle reached in and withdrew my weapon from beneath my right shoulder.

"You ah die ah here or you ah take us to Miki now ah," he said.

I looked around.

They had the drop on me.

No one was nearby. They had waited until the door behind me was closed and I was too far away to duck back in or yell for help.

I had no play here.

I had to think fast.

"You're not going to hurt her," I said.

He shook his head. "She ah family. Be-rong with us."

"What about her having to marry some old guy?" I asked.

"He ah very wealthy. Make ah good ah husband for dishonored girl. She ah be treated rike ah royarty."

It took me a moment to get that he was saying

royalty.

"But none of that matters if she doesn't want to marry him," I said, trying not to appear to be giving in too easily.

"Different ah customs. Take ah now or die."

Both gunsels pressed their respective barrels deeper into me, the one in the front just above my gunshot wound.

I flinched. And I wasn't faking.

"Okay," I said. "Swear to me as a man of honor you won't hurt her, and I'll take you to her."

"She ah not ah be hurt. Swear."

"And you won't hurt any of us," I said.

"Just want ah girl. No one get ah hurt if we ah get her."

"Swear to me on your word as an honorable man," I said.

"Swear."

I nodded. "Okay. I'll take you to her. I'll drive. You follow me."

He shook his head. "No."

They led me over to their car and put me in the passenger seat with one gunsel behind me and one beside me driving, both with their guns still pointed at me.

"Go up and take a right on eleventh," I said.

"You ah try and ah trick us, you ah die."

I nodded.

"Where ah is she?"

"We've been moving her around a lot. Different places. Different people watching her. We have an injured friend hiding in the hospital under a different name. She's in his room for a few hours this morning with another female friend—a reporter, Kay Hudson."

He nodded.

If they had been watching me they had probably seen Kay.

I didn't have a plan exactly. I was mostly making it all up as I went along, trying to give myself more time to come up with one. But at some point this morning Howell or Folsom were supposed to be interviewing Jeff and Kay. Maybe one or both of them were there now.

As we pulled up to Lisenby Hospital, I turned in the seat to face Miki's uncle.

"My friend is very, very ill," I said. "I don't want him disturbed and you gave me your word no one would get hurt. Remember what I've done for Miki and your family. I found her. I saved her. That's got to count for something."

He nodded. "It ah why you ah still arive."

"How do you want to do this?" I asked.

He studied the building. There was no obvious or easy way.

"He ah go with you," he said, nodding to the young gunsel beside him. "Any ah trouble, he ah shoot you. She ah not there, he ah shoot you. You ah try anything at ah all, he ah shoot you. Understand?"

"Yeah," I said, "anything happens and he ah shoot me."

He looked at the young guy beside him. "You ah wear hat and sun grasses. Keep ah hand on gun in ah pocket, pointed at ah his back ah whole time. Do not ah hesitate to ah shoot him."

He nodded and gave me a wolfish grin.

We walked through the front door of the hospital, just like he wasn't wanted by the United States government.

He was right behind me, so close that when I slowed I could feel the barrel of the weapon press into my lower back.

Passing through the lobby and waiting area, we continued past the nurses' station and down the long corridor to the right.

The hallway was empty, and I tried to figure out a way to make a move without getting shot, but couldn't come up with any.

When we neared Jeff's room, I only slowed slightly, and glanced in without turning my head in that direction.

No Howell. No Folsom. Only a sad, weary-looking Kay Hudson I wasn't even sure saw me.

"They said they might be moving him to another room," I said loudly. "We'll check where he was last night. If he's not there, I'll go ask the nurse where they moved him to."

"Try anything and I ah kill you," the soft voice said from behind me.

I turned to the left, to the room directly across from Jeff's, and tapped on the door loudly, hoping Kay would hear me and get help.

"Ray," I said. "Ray Parker. You in there?"

I opened the door and stepped a little ways inside, but the gunsel didn't follow.

When I turned around I knew why.

Both his hands were raised in the air, palms out in a gesture of surrender.

Behind him, Kay Hudson had a gun held up to the

back of his head.

I reached into his right coat pocket and withdrew the weapon he had pointed at me, then from his other I retrieved my gun.

"Thank you," I said to Kay.

"Pleasure," she said, and though I knew she meant it, the truth the one word contained was that she could find no pleasure in anything just now—maybe ever again.

"Have Howell and Folsom been by?" I asked.

She shook her head.

"I need to find a phone and call them."

"Only one is back down the hallway at the nurses' station," she said.

"Thanks. Come on."

I grabbed the gunsel by the arm and pulled him toward me, then followed him back up the hall.

I called Folsom from the phone at the nurses' station, and less than ten minutes later two police cars—his and another—had blocked in Miki's uncle's car, and the two men inside had surrendered without a single shot being fired.

"That could've gone a lot worse," Howell said.

I nodded. "Kay Hudson saved the day."

I had walked out with the gunsel I had gone in with, and beat cops were cuffing the three men and shoving them into the back of the two squad cars now present at the scene.

"This ah not ah over," Miki's uncle said to me.

"Never is," I said. "It never is."

"Get him out of here," Folsom said as he walked over to us. "Good work, Jimmy."

"Not me. Kay."

"While we're here," he said to Howell, "we might as well go ahead and interview her and Bennett."

Howell nodded.

"Treat her like the respected war correspondent and bereaved hero she is," I said.

Chapter 42

That night I did what Clip had been doing the past few nights—stood behind the door of the room across the hall from Saul's in the Marie Motel, staring through the peephole to see if the person leaving the notes threatening Freddy would show again.

My eyes burned. My body ached. My mind throbbed.

I had been exhausted and sore before I began. Now, after hours of standing and staring through the tiny hole, I was beyond bone-weary, but I had to do all I could to prevent the death of one of the best and most honorable men I knew.

Lauren was asleep in the bed behind me, her soft, continuous breathing as reassuring and rapturous a sound as any made in the middle of the night.

This was how I spent the last two nights before the big bout, but no one ever showed, no note was left, so I had no hope of finding and eliminating the threat before the fight started.

Each afternoon, while Lauren sat with Gladys in her

room, I had taken to sitting with Jeff in his.

I'm not sure he ever knew I was there.

Sad, vacant stare. Slack mouth slightly open. Drool cresting the corners of his mouth, dribbling down his chin. This truly talented athlete and sharp, insightful reporter was dead but not buried, reduced to an immobile infantile mound of semi-living cells.

The humanity and ignorance capable of this form of murder represented a monstrousness I had yet to encounter.

"Mr. Riley," Lady Bird Bennett said. "What are you doing here?"

She has just strode in like she owned the place—and probably did—immaculately dressed, wearing plenty that was banned or at least unavailable during the war.

"Wondering what kind of mother could do this to her son," I said.

"What? Love him enough to want to cure him?"

I shook my head. "It's not love. It's nothing like love. It has more in common with what the Nazis are doing than anything I've seen over here. And I've seen a lot."

"I think you need to go, Mr. Riley," she said. "My son needs his rest. I'm taking him home today."

I stood and stepped toward her. "You murdered your son," I said. "Worse. You killed him and let him live to experience every second of the torture involved in being what he is."

"You think what I did was wrong?" she asked.

"Wrong doesn't even begin it."

She nodded and gave me the coldest smile I'd ever been given. "Let me ask you this, you cheap dime-store detective. What can you do about it?"

I shook my head and shrugged. "I could shoot you in the face."

"Legally," she said. "What can you really do legally?"

I didn't say anything.

"I'll tell you," she said. "Nothing. Absolutely nothing."

She was right and we both knew it.

I looked back at Jeff.

I shook my head as the first tears began to well up in my tired eyes.

"He may never win another award for war reporting, may not ever box another single round of boxing," she said, "but he'll damn sure never commit another obscene act of perversion either. And I'd say that's a pretty fair exchange."

I patted Jeff's hand, then turned to leave.

When I reached the door, I looked back at her and said, "I ever do start shooting people in the face, yours'll be the first."

"From what I hear, you're a back shooter," she said. "And do you really want to say such things to a woman capable of this?" She nodded her head toward her once great now pathetic son.

Noah Mosely appeared in the doorway behind me. "Game, set, match to Lady Bird Bennett," he said. "Now run along, little peeper. Go pester those without means. We've had quite enough of you."

It was the day before the fight.

The Bay High School gym was empty except for Clip, Gus, me, and Saul.

Clip was over in the corner bouncing the speed bag about, the rhythmic back and forth sounding like Latin percussion. His hand speed and precision were amazing.

"Impressive," Saul said.

I nodded.

We were standing on the other side of the ring, nearly on the other side of the gym.

Gus emerged from the dressing room and started walking back over toward Clip, tape, scissors, and a water bottle in his hands.

Saul motioned him over.

"He's a natural, this one," Saul said, nodding toward Clip.

Gus nodded, looking across the way toward the speed bag. "Gots lots of natural ability," he said. "He quick. Tough. Good chin too."

"He got a shot?" Saul asked.

Gus frowned and shook his head. "Even if we had more time to train, to teach him boxing . . . even if we could get him some fights too . . . It's no good. Eye's too much a liability. Linderman's too skilled, too experienced not to exploit it."

Saul nodded slowly, knowingly, like all the man had done was confirm what he already knew.

Something inside me sank.

"With his chin," Gus said, "with his toughness and stubbornness . . ."

"Yeah?" Saul said, a hint of hope in his voice.

"He could take . . . an awfully bad beating . . . just keep gettin' up for more."

Saul nodded again, and again something inside me sank even deeper.

"Do that too much against a fighter like Linderman," Gus said, "he'll kill you."

David Howell showed up about an hour later.

Clip was in the ring with a sparring partner, but instead of sparring, Gus was having the man stand in various positions and walking Clip through what to do to counter what Linderman would do.

"What's going on here?" David said.

I told him.

He shook his head and looked at Clip, his gesture and expression conveying admiration not disapproval.

I told him about the threatening letters Freddy had been getting. "I'm gonna need some help protecting him," I added.

"You got it."

"Thanks."

We were quiet a while, watching Gus in the most quiet and unassuming way show his encyclopedic knowledge, insight, and understanding of boxing.

"Interviewed Jeff Bennett," he said. "With a lot of help from Kay. He doesn't say much and what he does doesn't make much sense. Unless he improves—and the doctor is doubtful he will much more—he'll be no help at all as a witness. Even if he were willing to do it, which he's not, the defense attorney would pick his teeth with him. They say he survived his ice pic lobotomy, but I wouldn't. I wouldn't say that at all."

Nothing he was saying surprised me, but it was still a blow.

"With Kay's help and the little I could get from him,

I've pieced together what I think happened," he said.

"What's that?"

"What we already knew or at least suspected. Bennett thought he could blackmail his mother with a story exposing her and some of her closest friends in various unethical and illegal activities. Leave him alone, let him be and do what he wants to and he won't print it. That sort of thing."

I nodded.

"He's in a room at the Dixie with the young man who was killed, Cecil Deets. A man he can't identify breaks in on them, tells Jeff he's a sick embarrassing deviant and is coming with him to get some help. The man has weapons. They fight him anyway. Cecil is killed. Jeff is knocked out and taken away. Wakes up in Dr. Delpy's sanatorium."

"You know who's behind it," I said.

"I do," he said. "We all do—including Folsom. No way we get her on this, but we'll keep watching, keep digging . . . Eventually we'll get her on something."

"All you been through and you're still an optimist," I said.

"You don't think we will?"

I shook my head.

"Because we're inept or corrupt?" he said.

"Neither," I said.

"I won't stop," he said.

"Good."

"I'll prove you wrong."

"I hope so," I said.

"Oh," he said. "Folsom's name was on the list 'cause Jeff believed he was the cleanest cop in town and would help him."

Chapter 43

"*This Nation in the past two years has become an active partner in the world's greatest war against human slavery,*" the president said, beginning his State of the Union Address to Congress. "*We have joined with like-minded people in order to defend ourselves in a world that has been gravely threatened with gangster rule. But I do not think that any of us Americans can be content with mere survival. Sacrifices that we and our allies are making impose upon us all a sacred obligation to see to it that out of this war we and our children will gain something better than mere survival.*"

Roosevelt's voice, blasted from the PA system set up for just that purpose, echoed through downtown, bouncing off the USO building and around the makeshift boxing ring until it was absorbed by the enormous crowd that had turned out for the match.

"*We are united in determination that this war shall not be followed by another interim which leads to new disaster, that we shall not repeat the tragic errors of ostrich isolationism—that we shall not repeat the excesses of the wild twenties when this Nation went for a joy ride on a roller coaster which ended in a tragic crash.*"

I was in Clip's corner, parading around as a cut man, but really providing security, the .38 under my right shoulder hidden by the cardigan sweater I was wearing with Fighting Freddy Freeman on the back.

David Howell and Folsom and a few other cops were roaming the crowd. Lauren and Miki looked through binoculars from the back of a pickup across the way. Everyone alert for anything suspicious that might identify the would-be assassin.

Besides Saul, Gus, and me, they were the only ones who knew that Fighting Freddy Freeman was actually Clipper Jones.

At a table ringside, the radio announcer calling the fight, a middle-aged man in a gray suit and fedora and burgundy bowtie known as Radio Red McCall, was saying, "It appears that Fighting Freddy Freeman overtrained for the fight, lost too much weight, and has somehow seriously injured his left eye. The bigger, sharper Linderman must outweigh the Negro fighter by over thirty pounds. Folks, don't go anywhere. This one won't last long."

As the ring announcer finished the introductions, I continued scouring the crowd, searching, scanning, trying to suss out who might have a weapon and ill intentions.

Near ringside I saw Corn Griffin, who a decade before had been the number two heavyweight contender in the world—at least until he met up with James J. Braddock at the Madison Square Garden Bowl in June of '34.

Born in Blountstown less than forty-five minutes away, Corn Griffin was considered a local, and his defeat by Braddock at the Garden when Braddock was considered washed-up and only given two days' notice for the fight was dismissed with the explanation that he hadn't taken the match seriously, had gone out drinking the night before and was still hung over.

When I looked back, seconds were out of the ring and the bout was beginning.

The bell sounded and Clip bounced out to meet Leonaldo Linderman, who charged across the ring toward him.

"Linderman storms out of his corner," Red said into his microphone. "He senses what all of us here at ringside do—Freddy's lights are halfway out already."

Linderman loaded up, obviously going for a one-punch knockout in the first seconds of the fight.

"Linderman's first punch is a looping right hook that barely misses," Red said. "He's swinging for the fences, folks. I could feel the force of that one down here."

Linderman led with his right because of Clip's left eye—something I was sure he would go to again and again as the fight went on.

Clip was moving and dancing, bouncing and bobbing about, avoiding the haymakers Lindermen was throwing. He wasn't able to throw much of anything himself and he landed even less, but he had yet to be hit, yet to taste leather or canvas.

All this continued throughout a first round that was mostly Linderman feeling Clip out and Clip just trying to survive.

Even this early in the bout, the crowd began to show its displeasure for what was a low-action, pedestrian fight.

Radio Red was saying, "The crowd is growing restless already. Some have already started a petition to change Freddy's name from Fighting to Dodging and Ducking."

The bell sounded. Round one was completed.

Clip came over and collapsed onto the small stool,

panting and wheezing.

As Gus began to coach him, I continued to search the crowd, and Roosevelt's voice could once again be heard through the PA.

"There are pests who swarm through the lobbies of the Congress and the cocktail bars of Washington, representing these special groups as opposed to the basic interests of the Nation as a whole. They have come to look upon the war primarily as a chance to make profits for themselves at the expense of their neighbors—profits in money or in terms of political or social preferment. Such selfish agitation can be highly dangerous in wartime. It creates confusion. It damages morale. It hampers our national effort. It muddies the waters and therefore prolongs the war."

Gus was saying, "He's loading up on you, trying to knock you out with every punch. Be faster. Hit him hard two times while he's pulling back them big arms of his."

Clip nodded, but was breathing too heavily to respond.

"You okay?" I asked.

He nodded, making eye contact with me to let me know he meant it.

The ding of the bell, and round two was underway.

"Again Linderman comes out swinging," Red said. "Charging out of his corner like a bull, throwing one bomb after another—a straight right, an overhand left, a right hook, followed by a left uppercut. Freddy is quick, bobbing, weaving, dancing around the bigger, slower man, but his arms and hands and shoulders are taking a beating, a brutal beating. And it'll all be for nothing if even one of Linderman's punches gets through."

Clip continued to move. The crowd continued to boo, some even beginning to throw popcorn and trash into the ring.

I tried to figure out what the killer was waiting for. Based on what he was seeing, did he think Clip would lose the fight all on his own and there would be no need to take him out? Was he waiting for a particular time or something to happen in the ring? Had the threats been hollow, meant only to intimidate, and so there would be no attempt to kill Clip at all?

"Freeman buys some real estate by bouncing off the rope and throwing several fast shots," Red said, "but gives it right back as Linderman once again smothers him."

Clip was still managing to avoid Linderman's biggest punches, but he was getting closer and closer to catching him.

And then he did.

"Freeman takes a left to the body and a hard right to the head," Red announced. "Linderman keeps cutting off the ring, stalking Freeman, finding him, going downstairs with some very hard body shots, then as Freeman brings his arms down, going to the head, sticking the jab . . . and . . . then . . . Down goes Freeman on a Linderman right hook."

Chapter 44

The whistles, yells, and claps from the crowd swelled, the bloodthirsty cheering deafening.

Linderman landed a perfectly placed right hook to Clip's jaw, just beneath his missing eye, and Clip went down hard, but somehow rolled on the canvas and popped right back up.

Which was a mistake.

Linderman was on him again, putting him right back down with right hook and left uppercut.

"Stay down," Gus yelled. "Get yourself together. Don't get up till seven or eight."

Or don't get up at all, I thought, but I knew that wasn't going to happen.

After a seven count, Clip climbed back to his feet, but before Linderman could cross the ring to finish him off, mercifully—or not—the bell rang.

Red was saying, "You could give Freeman three eyes. Wouldn't matter."

Between rounds, Clip tried to recover, Gus coached him as best he could, and I continued scanning the now raucous crowd.

On the PA, barely audible above the crowd, Roosevelt was saying, *"Overconfidence and complacency are among our deadliest enemies. Last spring—after notable victories at Stalingrad and in Tunisia and against the U-boats on the high seas—overconfidence became so pronounced that war production fell off. In two months, June and July, 1943, more than a thousand airplanes that could have been made and should have been made were not made. Those who failed to make them were not on strike. They were merely saying, 'The war's in the bag, so let's relax.' That attitude on the part of anyone—government or management or labor—can lengthen this war. It can kill American boys."*

Roosevelt's voice faded, seconds climbed out, the bell sounded, round three began.

Clip was obviously still wobbly. Linderman pressed his advantage, practically running across the ring and letting his hands go.

"Now Linderman is getting whatever he wants," Red said. "Whipping Freeman from pillar to post, landing some violent two- and three-punch combinations at will. In between, he's delivering some vicious body shots. I don't know how much more Freeman can take."

Somehow Clip stayed on his feet, stumbling about, falling away from the punches, leaning against the ropes, bouncing back into them.

Linderman kept coming. Clip, who seemed to be finding his feet again, blocked the worst of it with his arms and gloves and kept moving.

"Folks, Fighting Freddy Freeman may not be the boxer that Leonaldo Lights Out Linderman is, but he's got no shortage of heart. It may get him killed, but he's not going away easy."

Slowly, Clip gained a little ground, began throwing in

a little offense in between fending off Linderman.

"Freeman has picked up the pace a bit," Red said, "fighting off Linderman with two- and three-shot combinations. Freeman is not without some skill. He's okay. He's just not a big puncher, but he's fast . . . and there's a formula here for Freeman to get back in the fight. If he can keep up this pace, if he can continue to be the more active fighter, keep Linderman missing, keep avoiding those Lights Out shots . . . Freeman continues to keep the big puncher at bay, but how much longer can that last? There it is. Linderman snaps out a stiff jab and catches Freeman coming in. There's blood coming from the Negro's nose now."

And then just like before . . . Linderman landed a perfectly placed right hook on Clip's jaw, just beneath his blind spot. This one dropped Clip flat.

"Down goes Freeman," Red yelled into the mic.

The crowd erupted again.

Clip didn't move.

Stay down. Please stay down.

"Clear your head," Gus yelled. "Take your time. Get up when you ready."

Clip gave no indication he heard him—or could hear anyone. He had still yet to so much as twitch.

"It appears Freeman may be out cold," Red said.

The ref moved toward him just then, starting the ten count.

Before he reached him, Clip began pushing himself up off the canvas, his arms shaking from the effort.

He stood before the ref reached ten, but I wasn't sure he even knew where he was.

"Freeman is up on his feet," Red said.

Clip stumbled back into the corner where we were.

"That's enough, Cli—Freddy," I yelled. "You've done enough."

He shook his head.

Gus said, "Show me somethin', son, or I'm'a have to call it."

The ref wiped Clip's gloves on his shirt and said, "You want to continue?"

Clip nodded.

The ref backed out of the way.

And then the gunman made his move.

From across the ring, blocked mostly by the mammoth mound that was Linderman, a young, chubby, pale, pimply faced kid jumped up on the apron of the ring and pointed a pistol toward Clip.

I jumped toward the ring, missing the step and falling. Reaching up for the rope with my right hand, it wasn't until I missed grabbing it that I realized my hand was no longer there.

I hit the canvas hard, landing on my back, and began to spin.

I was useless.

I couldn't even stand, let alone draw my weapon and fire at the boy.

Clip, unaware of what was going on, began to take a step toward Linderman and the gunman behind him, aiding in his own assassination.

Reaching beneath the ropes with my left hand—the only one I had—I did the only thing I could. I grabbed Clip's ankle.

He was unsteady anyway, dead on his feet. It didn't take much. As he tried to move forward, I tripped him and he hit the canvas for a third and final time.

The gunman fired.

Missed everyone and everything.

Screams. Yells. Panic.

Linderman turned toward the sound that came from just behind him, snapping out a stiff left jab and a right hook that knocked the boy off the ring and sent him hard to the asphalt of Harrison below.

In an instant Howell and Folsom were on him, cuffing him, securing him in the roughest possible manner, though he was still out cold and probably would be for some time to come.

The crowd dispersed. The big bout was over. Linderman was declared the winner, but the greatest victory of the day went to Clip, hands down.

Someone turned up Roosevelt again, but nobody was listening.

"That is the way to fight and win a war—all out—and not with half an eye on the battlefronts abroad and the other eye and a half on personal, selfish, or political interests here at home."

"Bastard knew I was about to come back," Clip said. "Why he tried to shoot my ass when he did. Waited just a little longer, I'd'a won the fight."

I nodded.

We were standing near the ring. For the moment it was just the two of us.

"You saved my life," he said.

"I'm not sure that fat fucker could've actually hit you," I said. "Not an easy shot with a pistol."

"'Specially way I's bouncin'," he said.

"Oh," I said, "you were going to bob and weave around a bullet, huh?"

"You doubt it?"

I shook my head. "I don't doubt that you can do anything," I said. "Hell of a fight."

"Thanks for makin' sure it wasn't my last."

"Clip," I said, my voice thick and hoarse, "you're the best man I know. I feel so blessed to have you for a friend."

David Howell slowly walked over to us.

"Know who that was?" he asked.

We both shook our heads.

"Nobody," he said. "A nobody. Just some punk. Says he just hates niggers. Wants the next heavyweight to be white."

"Make him a everybody, not a nobody," Clip said.

Howell started to say something, then stopped.

He knew Clip was right. The scary thing about the kid with the gun wasn't that he was no one. It was that he could be anyone. The sickness he was infected with was a contagion carried by far too many among us, most of whom looked as hapless and harmless as the pale, pimply faced kid.

Chapter 45

A few days later, Lauren and I and Clip and Miki were walking down Harrison toward the water.

It was evening, dim duskiness fading to grayish blackness. Lights from stores blinked on and joined that of cars and streetlamps to keep the darkness at bay.

Lauren and I were holding hands, something Clip and Miki-dressed-as-Judy dared not do. We were all walking slowly, enjoying every step.

Clip, still spent and sore, was doing everything slowly these days.

We had just left the office and didn't know where we were going, but we didn't care. We were still here. We were together. All other considerations could wait.

Across the street, on the crowded sidewalk on the opposite side of Harrison, my old partner and former Pinkerton Ray Parker stood watching us, a quizzical expression on his face.

He was wearing the same outfit he had been when I had killed him.

"Ray?" I said.

"What?" Lauren said beside me.

"I thought I saw—"

"How's the eye, Freddy?" a young soldier passing by Clip said.

"You were gonna get him," his companion, also a young soldier, said.

"Who tried to shoot you?" the first one asked.

Neither boy stopped or even slowed, both gone before Clip could respond, carried along by the anonymous throng.

"Jimmy," a voice called from behind us. "Lauren."

We all stopped and turned to see Kay Hudson carrying a suitcase coming up behind us.

I glanced back across the street. Ray was gone. Had he been there at all? Were we here now?

"Hey Kay," Lauren said. "How are you?"

She frowned and shook her head. "Did you see the paper this morning?"

Kay had interviewed Clip as Freddy for the *News Herald*, giving him a chance to say even more of what mattered to him and giving her the chance to question what really happened to Jeff Bennett. Clip also took questions about Freddy's future and Kay included information about the assassination attempt and wrote eloquently about the culpability of the sick society that had fostered the shooter's racism and paranoia.

"She got it pulled," Kay said.

We all knew the *she* was Lady Bird Bennett.

"You expected anything different, you in the wrong profession," Clip said.

"Hoped, not expected," she said. "Figured they'd edit out what they didn't like. Never thought they'd scrap the whole thing. Anyway, I'm leaving in a little while.

Wanted to say goodbye."

"Where are you going?"

"To a better place than this," she said. "Back to the front, back to where enemies are easy to identify and come at you head-on."

I nodded.

"Just know when you over there, we be back here fightin' the battles on the home front," Clip said. "We not gonna let what happened to Becky and Jeff go . . . unaddressed."

Kay nodded and gave him a look that conveyed both gratitude and futility.

"I'm so sorry again," Lauren said. "For all that happened. For all you've been through."

Kay's eyes drifted down to our hands, which were still clasped.

"I told you," she said.

She was looking at me. I waited.

"Told you Becky and I weren't allowed to have it," she said. "To have love. To have what you two have."

Clip leaned forward a little. "You ain't the only one ain't allowed," he said, nodding toward Miki. "Truth is, world ain't big on lettin' no one have it."

"They're doing all right," she said, nodding toward me and Lauren.

"For how long?" he said.

I squeezed Lauren's hand.

"Hell, how long you think they had it?" Clip asked. "What you think they had to go through to get it? You really think they got long? Think anyone do?"

"Again," Lauren said, "we're very sorry. Wish we could've done more."

"I know," she said. "I'm sorry. I didn't mean I'm not happy for you two. I just meant . . . well, you know. And I know Clip's right. I know you don't have long."

Those were her final words. As soon as she delivered them, she turned and walked away from us, back the way she came, quickly vanishing into the throng.

But those weren't the final words on the subject.

As we turned and continued our walk, Lauren squeezed my hand even more tightly.

"As far as I'm concerned," she said, "we have forever."

And with that, tomorrow and tomorrow and tomorrow turned into forever.

About Michael Lister

Multi-award-winning novelist Michael Lister is a native Floridian best known for literary suspense thrillers and mysteries.

The Florida Book Review says that "Vintage Michael Lister is poetic prose, exquisitely set scenes, characters who are damaged and faulty," and Michael Koryta says, "If you like crime writing with depth, suspense, and sterling prose, you should be reading Michael Lister," while Publisher's Weekly adds, "Lister's hard-edged prose ranks with the best of contemporary noir fiction."

Michael grew up in North Florida near the Gulf of Mexico and the Apalachicola River in a small town world famous for tupelo honey.

Truly a regional writer, North Florida is his beat.

In the early 1990s, Michael became the youngest chaplain within the Florida Department of Corrections. For nearly a decade, he served as a contract, staff, then senior chaplain at three different facilities in the Panhandle of Florida—a unique experience that led to his first novel, 1997's critically acclaimed, POWER IN THE BLOOD. It was the first in a series of popular and celebrated novels featuring ex-cop turned prison chaplain, John Jordan. Of the John Jordan series, Michael Connelly says, "Michael Lister may be the author of the most unique series running in mystery fiction. It crackles with tension and authenticity," while Julia Spencer-Fleming adds, "Michael Lister writes one of the most ambitious and unusual crime fiction series going. See what crime fiction is capable of."

Michael also writes historical hard-boiled thrillers, such as THE BIG GOODBYE, THE BIG BEYOND, and THE BIG HELLO featuring Jimmy "Soldier" Riley, a PI in Panama City during World War II (www.SoldierMysteries.com). Ace Atkins calls the "Soldier" series "tough and violent with snappy dialogue and great atmosphere . . . a suspenseful, romantic and historic ride."

Michael Lister won his first Florida Book Award for his literary novel DOUBLE EXPOSURE. His second Florida Book Award was for his fifth John Jordan novel BLOOD SACRIFICE.

Michael also writes popular and highly praised columns on film and art and meaning and life, that can be found at www.WrittenWordsRemain.com.

His nonfiction books include the "Meaning" series: THE MEANING OF LIFE, MEANING EVERY MOMENT, and THE MEANING OF LIFE IN MOVIES.

Lister's latest literary thrillers include DOUBLE EXPOSURE, THUNDER BEACH, BURNT OFFERINGS, SEPARATION ANXIETY, and A CERTAIN RETRIBUTION.